MW01245425

ALL EAGLES ARE SUPPOSED TO SOAR

ALL EAGLES ARE SUPPOSED TO SOAR

Positive Teachers Give Their Students Wings

Janice Kathleen Farley

Writers Club Press
New York Lincoln Shanghai

All Eagles Are Supposed to Soar
Positive Teachers Give Their Students Wings

All Rights Reserved © 2002 by Janice Kathleen Farley

No part of this book may be reproduced or transmitted in any form or by any means, graphic, electronic, or mechanical, including photocopying, recording, taping, or by any information storage retrieval system, without the written permission of the publisher.

Writers Club Press
an imprint of iUniverse, Inc.

For information address:
iUniverse, Inc.
2021 Pine Lake Road, Suite 100
Lincoln, NE 68512
www.iuniverse.com

ISBN: 0-595-26241-4

Printed in the United States of America

This book is dedicated to:

My husband Elmer Farley—
Thank you for love and empowering support.

My daughter-in-law Rhoda Zipperer—
Thank you for "angel" inspiration.

My daughter Robyn Reed and my son Trae Zipperer

My parents Paul and Myrtle Surgnier

My grandchildren Noah, August, Jack, and Kolby—
Seth, Kiersten, and Tristan

My brother Steven Surgnier, M.D.

My mother-in-law Reva Farley

My former students

In loving memory of my grandparents Paul and Blandena Surgnier

In loving memory of my student Anthony (Tony) Oliver—O.H.S.,
Class of 1986

If *all* teachers were positive teachers,
all students would "mount up with wings as eagles."

Contents

Positive Teachers Smile

Positive Teachers Use Positive Language

Positive Teachers Stimulate Students

Positive Teachers Help Students

Positive Teachers Are Patient

Positive Teachers Are Compassionate

Positive Teachers Encourage Students

Preface

Being a positive teacher isn't an easy mission. It isn't easy to teach stimulating lessons all day long. It isn't easy to smile all day long. It isn't easy to be patient, encouraging, attentive, motivating, inspiring, and compassionate all day long. It isn't easy to be energetic and enthusiastic all day long. It isn't easy to stimulate students to succeed.

Passing out worksheets is much easier than teaching a lesson. Venting aggravation is much easier than practicing patience. Being apathetic is much easier than being active and ardent. Reprimanding students is much easier than encouraging students. Disciplining students is much easier than motivating and inspiring students.

Ignoring students' personal problems is much easier than intervening and offering assistance. Handing out criticism is much easier than handing out hope. Complaining is much easier than seeking a solution. Giving up is much easier than persevering. Failing students is much easier than stimulating them to succeed.

Certainly it's easier to be a negative teacher than a positive teacher. Certainly there is no monetary gain in being a positive teacher—negative teachers and positive teachers are paid the same salary. Certainly there are no raises, perks, or promotions for positive performance in the teaching profession. But a positive teacher will live with the perpetual wealth and reward of personal fulfillment that comes from touching the future with a positive impression—empowering students to become what they dream of becoming.

Positive teachers give their students wings.

Acknowledgments

I want to thank those people whose positive words have inspired me and influenced a positive difference in my life—particular teachers, family members, friends, colleagues, school administrators, and others.

Of all the positive words I've heard in my lifetime, one statement stands out as the most positively powerful—"*Always* say something positive" (Victor Gibbons, a school police officer and adjunct teacher).

Victor Gibbon's statement exemplifies the essence of positive teaching: If *all* teachers would *always* say something positive, *all* students would be stimulated to succeed.

A special thank-you to Diane Oliver for her positive assistance.

Introduction

"…they shall mount up with wings as eagles…"

—Isaiah 40:31

All babies, toddlers, and pre-schoolers are bright—ask any parent or grandparent. They won't hesitate to present proof of their children's/grandchildren's intelligence. They won't hesitate to tell you that they believe their children's/grandchildren's bright mentality will generate exceptional scholastic success; and ultimately, exceptional life success. But reality confirms that a majority of all of these bright children will achieve no more than average status as students; and more often than not, they will become average status adults. Reality confirms that many bright children will fail in school; and many of them will fail in life.

While several factors play an influential role in affecting a child's future—nurturing, environment, socio-economics—a primary factor is the influence of their teachers. Positive teachers affect positive futures; negative teachers affect negative futures.

On a recent visit to Washington, DC, I saw large numbers of homeless people living in city parks, begging on the streets. With few exceptions, these homeless people, mostly young men, looked strong and healthy. My stepson told me that one particular young man had been sitting on the same park bench for four years. No doubt, all of these homeless people—as babies, toddlers, and pre-schoolers—were thought to be bright. No doubt, their parents and grandparents were certain that their bright mentality would generate success in life.

So what happened that these bright children became adults sleeping on park benches, soliciting handouts as their source of sustenance? Some people believe the homeless lifestyle is a product of innate indolence. Some believe it's attributed to alcohol or drug addiction. Some believe homelessness is a consequence of long-term unemployment. But I believe the majority of homeless people are extreme examples of used-to-be bright children who were never stimulated to succeed. I believe that at the core of their life failure is a history of scholastic failure affected by negative teachers.

Fifty percent of American welfare recipients do not have a high school diploma. If *all* students were stimulated to succeed—if *all* students graduated from high school, empowered with knowledge, skills, and self-esteem—I believe welfare would, for the most part, cease to exist.

Eighty-two percent of the two million prisoners in the United States today are high school dropouts. If *all* of these one million six hundred forty thousand people had been stimulated to succeed in school, I believe a large majority of them would not be living behind bars today.

In the United States, over half a million students per year (about three thousand per day) drop out of school. A high school guidance counselor once told me, "We can't save them *all*." I believe we can.

Some years ago a family friend dropped out of high school because of chronic academic failure, and opted for a GED. After attending a GED study course, he took the exam, but he failed the English segment of the exam. He asked me to tutor him before taking the exam again.

Following four hours of intense tutoring on a Saturday afternoon, this young man took the GED exam the next week and passed the English segment with a very high score, the highest score in his exam group. Four hours of one-on-one academic instruction punctuated with praise and encouragement accomplished what four years of high school English classes, special academic programs, and a GED study course had not.

This young man had failed to learn in school, not because he wasn't bright—he was exceptionally bright to learn advanced grammar in a four hour class—but because he had been a victim of negative teaching. As he explained it, "I never had any teachers who helped me."

My oldest grandson was one of the brightest young children I've ever seen. His cognizance, verbal communication skill, creativity, and physical coordination were extraordinary. Everyone in our family agreed that this child would excel in school. All of us were stunned when his kindergarten teacher called a conference shortly after school commenced, and announced that he appeared to be a challenged student.

In first grade and second grade, my grandson continued to struggle academically. In third grade, the SLD program was recommended, but my daughter said she would absolutely not agree to it. She told the school administrators that she would tutor her son day and night if necessary, but he wasn't going to be placed in SLD which could stigmatize him for life.

In fourth grade, a positive teacher stimulated my grandson to succeed. For the first time, he liked school. But fifth grade, sixth grade, and seventh grade, the threat of failure loomed over him each school year. And finally, the threat became reality, and he failed eighth grade.

That summer my grandson came to stay with us for two weeks, and I tutored him a few hours every day. I used a motivational book as a textbook to tutor him in grammar, reading comprehension, composition, and critical thinking. I employed every positive teaching strategy I had ever exercised when I taught high school English. I mentored him in goal structuring, personal organization, and success postures. I praised him and encouraged him.

My grandson repeated eighth grade and made all A's and B's. In his freshman year of high school, he also achieved academic success. Now in his sophomore year, he is still succeeding. My grandson is contemplating attending college after graduation.

Last summer a challenged high school student in a neighboring county shot himself the day before school commenced. "Why did you do this?" his father cried as he held him, waiting for the ambulance to arrive. "I didn't want to go back to school," the wounded boy answered.

Scores of students, *all* of them bright, don't want to go to school because of the pain they suffer from nonsuccess. Scores of students, *all* of them bright, act out their pain and frustration in the form of negative behavior. Scores of students, *all* of them bright, turn to drugs and alcohol for relief and escape, some suicide. Scores of students, *all* of them bright, drop out of school each year. Scores of students, *all* of them bright, are scarred for life because of mental and emotional injuries suffered in school. Scores of students, *all* of them bright, never reach their potential in life because they weren't stimulated to succeed in school.

On the bulletin board of the first classroom in which, as a new teacher, I taught high school English, I pinned a poster—"What you can dream, you can become"—a statement that reflected my heart's conviction that *all* students can be stimulated to succeed.

Over the course of my teaching career, I stimulated many students to succeed, and many I did not. The primary difference between my students who succeeded and my students who didn't, and *all* of them were bright, was the difference between my positive teaching postures and my negative teaching postures.

The primary difference between every student who succeeds and every student who doesn't, and *all* of them are bright, is the difference between students being taught by positive teachers and students being taught by negative teachers.

Positive teachers employ stimulating teaching strategies; negative teachers subject students to academic tedium. Positive teachers help students; negative teachers label students. Positive teachers teach students; negative teachers teach curriculum.

Positive teachers are innovative; negative teachers resist new ideas. Positive teachers are positive role models; negative teachers model negative attitudes and behaviors. Positive teachers are personable; negative teachers are aloof.

Positive teachers are compassionate; negative teachers are condescending. Positive teachers listen; negative teachers turn away. Positive teachers are patient; negative teachers are quick-tempered.

Positive teachers inspire students; negative teachers intimidate students. Positive teachers praise; negative teachers criticize. Positive teachers practice behavior modification; negative teachers administer punishment.

Positive teachers smile; negative teachers frown. Positive teachers encourage; negative teachers discourage. Positive teachers are flexible; negative teachers are rigid. Positive teachers don't waste instructional time; negative teachers assign busywork.

Positive teachers express enthusiasm; negative teachers express indifference. Positive teachers motivate students; negative teachers suppress students. Positive teachers use positive language; negative teachers use negative language.

Positive teachers persevere; negative teachers give up. Positive teachers care; negative teachers are unconcerned. Positive teachers nurture students; negative teachers neglect students. Positive teachers empower students; negative teachers fail students.

If *all* teachers were positive teachers, *all* students would be stimulated to succeed.

All Eagles Are Supposed to Soar is a story inspired by my experiences and observations as a teacher. Names and characters are fictitious. Any resemblance to actual places, events, or persons, living or dead, is coincidental.

POSITIVE TEACHERS SMILE

CHAPTER 1

❀

On a sunny mid-August morning, fifteen hundred students crossed the threshold of Heritage High, home of the Eagles. The smell of fresh paint and floor wax permeated the corridors and classrooms. A shrill bell broadcast the beginning of a new school year.

Tenured English teacher Laura Nelson, a trim woman with dark, silver streaked hair, assigned grammar textbooks after she called the roll.

"Read chapter one, parts of speech; and answer the review questions at the end of the chapter," she instructed her general English seniors. "And no talking!" Her dark eyes flashed a warning of infraction consequences.

While her students worked on their assignment, Laura scanned faculty memos. She scowled when she read a note from the new principal Leon Williams: "Please meet with me after school today regarding 'first year teacher support' duty."

"First year teacher support", just the duty I don't want, especially if I have to deal with that new English teacher Emily Parker! She recalled Miss Parker's pretentious statement when Mr. Williams asked first

year teachers to share their teaching aspirations at the pre-planning faculty meeting: "I aspire to stimulate *all* of my students to succeed."

Laura snickered, thinking of algebra teacher Tom Edwards' comment: "Well, 'rots of ruck' to you, Miss Parker!"

"Excuse me." Julie Johnson, a slender, auburn haired girl, stood in front of Laura's desk.

"What?" Laura said.

"I don't understand some of the parts of speech."

"You're a senior and you don't understand parts of speech?"

"I don't understand adverbs and prepositions," Julie said.

"Then I suggest you reread those sections in chapter one," Laura said.

Julie returned to her desk, opened her textbook, and tried to grasp what she read, but thoughts of Timothy continued to impair her comprehension.

At the conclusion of class, Laura wrote on the board: "Homework—read chapter two, parts of a sentence; answer the review questions at the end of the chapter."

"Homework the first day?" Chad Bernelli protested.

Laura glared at the brown haired, blue-eyed boy wearing a red and white varsity football jersey emblazoned with an eagle. "Homework *every* day."

Emily Parker, a willowy, blonde haired young woman, opened her classroom door when the bell signaled the end of her first hour planning period. She stood outside her doorway and greeted her basic skills English students with a smile and words of welcome.

"Cool!" students chorused as they stepped into Emily's classroom and saw the windows valanced with red and white steamers, and a glittery banner—All Eagles are supposed to soar!—strung across the top of the chalkboard.

"Very cool!" a burly boy touched the outspread wings of a ceramic eagle perched on Emily's desk.

"Today we're going to review four of the eight parts of speech, the system we use to identity words by function," Emily addressed her freshmen students after she introduced herself and called the roll.

"Our school's symbol, the American eagle, will be our point of focus in reviewing nouns, pronouns, adjectives, and verbs," Emily said.

"A noun names a person, place, thing, quality, or idea," she explained as she wrote on the board. "The word eagle is a noun because it's the name of a bird. What common noun names an idea we associate with an eagle?"

"Freedom," the burly boy Eddie said.

"Yes!" Emily said.

"A pronoun is a substitute word for a noun. What pronoun could be substituted for the noun eagle?" Emily asked.

"It," Samantha, a redheaded girl wearing wire rimmed glasses, said.

"Correct!" Emily smiled.

"An adjective modifies, describes, a noun," Emily said. "The word American is an adjective when used to describe an eagle."

"And it's a noun when it refers to a person, right?" Jackson, a boy with a shaved head and gold hoop earrings in both ears, interjected.

"Right!" Emily smiled.

"A verb denotes action, or a state of being." Emily pointed at the banner above the chalkboard. "What's the 'elevating' action verb in this statement?"

"Soar!" several students answered in unison.

"Why did you capitalize eagles?" Amber, a round faced, heavyset girl, asked.

"Because I'm referring to all of you Heritage High students," Emily said. "Proper nouns—nouns that name specific person, places, or things—are capitalized."

"So you're saying we're supposed to fly?" Tracy, a thin, dark haired girl, sneered.

Emily smiled at the dark haired girl dressed in bell-bottom jeans, an oversized t-shirt, and sandals. "You're Eagles, aren't you?"

As her students left class at the end of second period, Emily passed out wing-shaped lapel pins that she had solicited from an airline.

"I don't want no dumb pin," Tracy snapped.

"Eagles need wings," Emily said.

"I don't need no wings to fly out of this school forever when I turn sixteen December twenty-first!"

"Why do you want to quit school?" Emily asked.

"Because I'm tired of failing. I'm already two years behind."

"If you could be a successful student, would you stay in school?"

"Me, a successful student? Impossible!"

"All things are possible." Emily smiled. "Would you be willing to stay after school, say an hour every day, if you could become a successful student?"

"You're gonna help me be a successful student?"

"Yes, I'm going to help you be a successful student."

"Why do you care about helping me?" Tracy's voice quavered.

Emily's green eyes sparkled. "I believe all Eagles are supposed to soar!"

Maybe I can be a successful student, Tracy Daniels pondered as her third period math teacher passed out textbooks. *Miss Parker said all things are possible.*

Tracy fastened the wing-shaped lapel pin to her t-shirt. She looked out the classroom windows at fluffy white clouds floating against a background of bright blue sky and felt hope stir in her heart.

Julie Johnson, her slender body bowed forward by the burden of a faded blue backpack, stood in Laura Nelson's doorway after school.

"Excuse me, Mrs. Nelson?"

Laura frowned at the auburn haired girl from her first period class. "What?"

"I need help with the homework assignment. I studied chapter two during lunch, but I still don't understand subject complements."

Laura picked up her tote bag. "I don't have time to help you. I have a meeting with the principal."

"Could you help me after your meeting? I could wait for you."

Laura ignored the imploring petition that Julie's brown eyes expressed. "I said I don't have time to help you."

"You'll be Emily Parker's support teacher this semester, Mrs. Nelson," Leon Williams said. "I want my support teachers to be available to answer questions and assist with any problems that first year teachers might encounter; and serve as mentors to our first year teachers."

"Mentors? I don't recall mentorship as a facet of support teacher duty, Mr. Williams."

"I think it's important that first year teachers have an experienced teacher coach them, offer constructive criticism regarding their teaching objectives," Leon said.

"I met with our new teachers yesterday and asked them to write synopses of their primary teaching objectives—one synopsis biweekly that they will submit to their support teacher who will submit a copy to me. As Miss Parker's mentor, you're to critique her primary teaching objectives and offer feedback. So please talk to her before you leave school today—she's expecting you—and schedule a time that the two of you can meet for biweekly conferences, beginning next week."

Leon stood and extended his hand. "Hope you have a good semester, Mrs. Nelson!"

Good semester? I haven't had a good day in sixteen years, she frowned at the tall, dark skinned new principal.

Tracy and Emily sat side by side at Emily's desk. Tracy picked up a picture frame standing beside the ceramic eagle. "Who's the cute guy?" she asked, looking at the photo of a blonde haired boy.

"My brother Todd."

"How old's your brother?" Tracy said.

Emily's eyes misted. "He would have been twenty-one."

Laura walked into Emily's classroom as Tracy was leaving at three-thirty. "See you tomorrow!" Tracy smiled at Emily, and then scowled at Laura.

"That girl's a delinquent," Laura snorted after Tracy had stepped out of the classroom.

"Delinquent?" Emily said.

"Last spring semester when I had in-school suspension duty sixth period, she was in there at least one day a week for some sort of negative behavior."

"Tracy's a challenged student," Emily said. "Her negative behavior is most probably a symptom of her pain."

Laura frowned. "Pain?"

"The pain of not succeeding in school," Emily answered. "Challenged students…"

"I'm not here to discuss challenged students," Laura huffed. "I'm here to schedule a conference with you next week. Mr. Williams said he informed you of the teaching objective synopses you're supposed to submit to me biweekly."

"So you're Laura Nelson, my support teacher?"

"Yes, I'm Laura Nelson. Put your first synopsis in my faculty box Monday morning, and we'll meet Monday after school. That will be the biweekly schedule."

"May we meet before school? I'll be tutoring Tracy, and possibly other challenged students, every day after school."

"Miss Parker, I'm not willing to sacrifice my personal time. We're paid to work an hour after school; we're not paid to work before school."

"I understand," Emily said. "But it's imperative that I give extra instructional time to students like Tracy Daniels. Tracy's failed two grade levels. She needs positive attention. With support and encouragement, challenged students can become successful students."

"Students like Tracy Daniels are not going to succeed no matter how much time you spend helping them."

Emily smiled. "I believe they will."

Laura glared at Emily. "Miss Parker, I'll see you next Monday *afternoon.*"

POSITIVE TEACHERS
USE
POSITIVE LANGUAGE

CHAPTER 2

❀

"Read chapter seven, subject-verb agreement; and answer the review questions at the end of the chapter," Laura instructed her first period seniors the second Monday morning of the semester.

"Reading chapters and answering questions every day is boring," Chad Bernelli asserted.

Laura frowned. "I'm not here to entertain you people."

"But aren't you here to teach us?"

Laura's face flushed. "Chad Bernelli, you can report for detention tomorrow afternoon!"

"Detention? Why?"

"Because you're insolent."

"I'm honest," he responded.

"Two days' detention!" her voice bounced off the classroom walls.

Laura sat down at her desk; her heart raced, her head pounded. *Every year is harder to tolerate—more students, more stress, more demands. And support teacher duty!* She snatched up the synopsis that Emily Parker had hand delivered:

Positive Conviction

"If you can believe, all things are possible..."

—Mark 9:23

Objective: I will sustain faith that *all* students, regardless of challenges, can be stimulated to succeed.

Stimulating all students to succeed begins with a personal conviction that *all* students *can* succeed, that there are no exceptions or limitations that can thwart the power of *positive* teaching—teaching postures and strategies polarized toward academic victory.

Teacher Anne Sullivan believed her student Helen Keller, blind and deaf since babyhood, could realize academic success. She polarized her teaching postures and strategies toward that victory, and her critically challenged student learned to read and write and speak.

When I encounter academically challenged students, I will remember how many times Anne Sullivan must have signed the word *water* before her student Helen Keller comprehended an intellectual perception of the word *water*. I will remember that Anne Sullivan did not give up, but pushed forward believing that her student, who could not see nor hear, could learn to read and write and speak.

Emily Parker

If you can believe, all things are possible? You're a dreamer, Miss Parker! Laura stuffed Emily's synopsis in her tote bag. She stood, stepped to the board, and wrote a list of twenty vocabulary words.

"Your homework assignment," she told her class, pointing at the words on the board. "Define the words, writing complete dictionary definitions for each one."

Her vision blurred with tears, Julie tried to copy the vocabulary words. *Timothy would have been sixteen today. He would have wanted a chocolate cake with chocolate frosting, and chocolate ice cream. Timothy loved chocolate. He loved birthdays—candles, balloons, and party hats.*

She still couldn't believe that Timothy had died. Surely she'd wake up and realize this was a nightmare. Surely it couldn't be true that a boy so full of love and life could die of a heart attack at fifteen years old. *But it is true,* a river of tears ran down Julie's face.

Chad didn't really know Julie Johnson, and he didn't know why she was crying, but he reached across the aisle and stroked her hand in sympathy for whatever reason she was distressed.

"Thank you," Julie whispered, clutching Chad's hand.

Second period, Emily wrote ten vocabulary words and definitions on the board. "Learning new words strengthens comprehension and communication skills," she told her class.

"Most teachers make us look up the definitions in the dictionary," Jackson said.

Emily smiled. "All of you have probably had enough practice doing that."

"Ya got that right!" Jackson said.

"Yeah," all the students agreed.

"We're going to make vocabulary flash cards today," Emily said.

"Is that why all the magazines and art stuff's on your desk?" Samantha asked.

"Yes," Emily answered. "I'd like you to find magazine pictures that visually express each of the words and definitions on the board. Clip the pictures, glue them on construction paper, and write the corresponding word and definition below your picture. The pictures will help you remember the words and definitions."

Emily picked up a magazine. "For example, your first vocabulary word is the adjective *assertive* which means positive, confident." She thumbed through the magazine. "He looks *assertive,* positive and confident," she said, showing her students a picture of a smiling salesman in a car advertisement.

"Making vocabulary flash cards sounds like fun!" Melanie, a petite girl with bobbed blonde hair, said.

Emily smiled. "Learning can be fun."

Tracy and three other students waited in the corridor while Emily and Laura met for their Monday afternoon conference.

Laura looked at Emily's desktop. "Were you teaching English or art today?"

"Vocabulary." Emily handed Laura a stack of flash cards.

Laura frowned. "You have time to cut and paste in class?"

"I believe creative activities help students learn," Emily said.

"These kids are in high school, not pre-school," Laura said.

"All students can benefit from creative learning activities," Emily said.

"*All* seems to be a popular word with you, Miss Parker. *All* things are possible, *all* students can be stimulated to succeed." Laura's eyes blazed with contempt. "Do you really believe that *all* students can be stimulated to succeed?"

"Yes." Emily smiled.

Laura sat in her classroom, waiting for the three-thirty bell to ring; waiting to leave to pick up Michael at his school across town. *Michael should be here, not there. Michael should be playing varsity football this year. Michael should have a drivers license now. Michael should be planning his future—what college he wants to attend, what profession he wants to pursue.*

POSITIVE TEACHERS
STIMULATE STUDENTS

CHAPTER 3

❈

The fourth Monday morning of the semester, Laura passed out graded vocabulary tests. "Julie Johnson," she called.

Julie came forward, smiling. "Hope I made a good grade this time. I studied hard."

"You failed again," Laura said.

"How could anyone pass?" Chad said.

"What's that supposed to mean?" Laura frowned.

"You don't review the definitions with us," he said.

"Seniors shouldn't need reviews," Laura retorted.

"But we don't know which definitions to study," Chad argued. "The dictionary lists several definitions for lots of the words."

"Then I suggest you learn *all* of the definitions listed for each word," Laura said.

While her students analyzed sentence types in a grammar book exercise, Laura read Emily Parker's second synopsis:

Positive Attention

"The future is purchased by the present."

—Samuel Johnson

Objective: I will stimulate *all* of my students to succeed.

We are a significant part of our students' future. The success, or failure, they experience in our class will influence their life experience.

We have nine months, one hundred and eighty days, to motivate students to succeed. The final bell on the last day of a school year tolls a solemn announcement that our active role as our students' teacher has been terminated. Regrets cannot be redeemed after the final bell; failures cannot be resurrected. Those students who leave our classroom without having realized success take us with them, for we are a part of their failure.

We must heed the urgency of our mission to motivate all of our students to succeed. Make every day count. Remain conscious of the time span between the first bell and the last, one hundred and eighty days. We will not receive more time. We must teach with a fervor of *positive* attention that when the final bell tolls, it reverberates a tone of success for *all* students.

Emily Parker

Motivate all kids to succeed? Not possible, Miss Parker. Not for Michael.

"Motor imaging—expressing the meanings of words with gestures—can help you learn new words," Emily told her second period students.

She pointed to the first vocabulary word and definition on the board. "Melanie, what gesture would you convey to express the meaning of the adjective *eminent*—tall, elevated?"

Melanie rose from her desk and stood on tiptoe.

"Very *eminent*, Melanie!" Emily smiled.

She pointed to the second vocabulary word and definition on the board. "Nathan, what gesture would you convey to express the meaning of the noun *acclaim*—approval, praise?"

Nathan, a quarterback on the freshmen football team, clapped loudly.

"Very demonstrative *acclaim*, Nathan!" Emily smiled.

"Who would like to convey a gesture for the meaning of the third word, the verb *empower*—enable, promote?"

Tracy stood, extended her arms, and flapped them up and down like wings.

"Very *empowering*, Tracy!" Emily smiled.

"Now I'd like you to choose partners and practice motor imaging the meanings of the other seven vocabulary words and definitions listed on the board," Emily instructed.

"Miss Parker, I overheard an alarming comment in the cafeteria line today," Laura said that afternoon. "A student was telling another student that you don't give homework assignments. Is that true?"

"Yes, it's true. I don't assign homework."

Laura frowned. "Homework is a traditional academic discipline, Miss Parker."

"I don't aspire to be a traditional teacher, Mrs. Nelson. I aspire to be a positive teacher. Sending students home with academic assignments and no academic assistance does not reflect positive academic attention that stimulates students to succeed."

Tracy Daniels, Stephen Bernelli, Brittney Anderson, and Ricky Reinhardt filed into Emily's classroom when Laura walked out.

"That Mrs. Nelson was a witch in in-school suspension last year," Tracy said to Emily.

"Mrs. Nelson's my brother's English teacher," Stephen, a tall boy with burred hair, said. "Chad told me that she won't explain anything in class. And she's real rude!"

"Sounds like my math teacher," Brittney, a slim, dark skinned girl, said.

"Sounds like my science teacher," Ricky, a husky, blonde haired boy, said.

"My brother's afraid he's going to fail English this semester," Stephen said.

"If *all* teachers were positive teachers, *no one* would fail!" Tracy said.

After Tracy, Stephen, Brittney, and Ricky left at three-thirty, Emily sat at her desk by the classroom wall of windows and pondered a poem that her heart had memorized:

"How a Child Learns"

If a child lives with criticism, he learns to condemn.
If a child lives with hostility, she learns to fight.
If a child lives with ridicule, he learns to be shy.
If a child lives with shame, she learns to feel guilty.
If a child lives with tolerance, he learns to be patient.
If a child lives with encouragement, she learns confidence.
If a child lives with praise, he learns to appreciate.
If a child lives with fairness, she learns justice.
If a child lives with security, he learns to have faith.
If a child lives with approval, she learns to like herself.
If a child lives with acceptance and friendship, he learns to find love
in the world.

Emily looked out the windows—*And if a child lives with positive teaching, he learns to soar!*

POSITIVE TEACHERS
HELP STUDENTS

CHAPTER 4

❀

The sixth Monday morning of the semester, Laura checked weekend homework assignments while her first period students read a short story in their literature textbook and answered questions at the end of the story.

"Mrs. Nelson, what's imagery?" a student said.

"What's metaphor?" another student chimed.

Laura frowned. "Look in the glossary!"

Julie raised her hand. "Glossary? What's glossary?"

Laura glared at her. "What chance do you have of passing senior English if you don't even know what a glossary is?"

Chad tapped his desktop to draw Julie's attention, and pointed at the glossary in the back of the literature textbook.

Julie smiled wanly, blinking back tears.

Second period, Emily read aloud from the ninth grade literature textbook:

"The Road Not Taken"
—Robert Frost

Two roads diverged in a yellow wood,
And sorry I could not travel both
And be one traveler, long I stood
And looked down one as far as I could
To where it bent in the undergrowth:

Then took the other, as just as fair,
And having perhaps the better claim,
Because it was grassy and wanted wear;
Though as for that the passing there
Had worn them really about the same,

And both that morning equally lay
In leaves no step had trodden black.
Oh, I kept the first for another day!
Yet knowing how way leads on to way,
I doubted if I should ever come back.

I shall be telling this with a sigh
Somewhere ages and ages hence;
Two roads diverged in a wood, and I—
I took the one less traveled by,
And that has made all the difference.

"*Theme* is the underlying meaning—the message—that a literary work is communicating," Emily said, writing her statement on the board.

"What *theme*, what message, do you think Robert Frost is communicating in his poem about choosing one of two roads to travel?" she asked.

"Choosing a direction in life," Juan, a stocky, dark haired boy, answered.

"He's telling us to choose a path that feels right for us," Samantha said.

"He's telling us that choosing a path that feels right to us will make a positive difference in our lives," Eddie said.

"What bright students you are!" Emily's smile wrapped around the room. "*All* of you!"

Laura Nelson, Tom Edwards, Sandy Turner, and Gayle Stone drank coffee and fraternized in the faculty lounge during their second hour planning period.

"This morning one of my American history students asked me where Pearl Harbor is!" Sandy laughed. "Can you believe a high school junior could be so ignorant?"

"I can believe it," Tom said. "Lots of my algebra students don't know basic math!"

"Yeah, some of my science students aren't too bright," Gayle said. "But bright or not, a lot of them could improve their grades if they stopped daydreaming during class. Some of my students just sit and stare out the window all period."

Laura snickered. "Maybe they're focused on personal pain. According to our new English teacher Emily Parker, personal pain is a major cause of poor academic performance."

She extracted Emily's third synopsis from her tote bag and read to her colleagues:

Positive Compassion

"If I can stop one heart from breaking, I shall not live in vain."
—Emily Dickinson

Objective: I will be a compassionate teacher.

Great numbers of students are in distress: learning disabilities, emotional disorders, dysfunctional families, poverty, physical and mental abuse, neglect, rejection, deprivation, loneliness, failure, fear, anxiety, ridicule, illness, physical handicaps, disappointment—and other personal pain that affects academic performance.

Expecting students to focus their attention on academic instruction when they are focused on their pain is an unrealistic expectation. Students who are sick cannot concentrate on learning and succeeding. Students who suffer from abuse, neglect, or deprivation cannot concentrate on learning and succeeding. Students who are hungry for food, love, acceptance, or attention cannot concentrate on learning and succeeding. A student who is angry, humiliated, discouraged, or depressed, cannot concentrate on learning and succeeding.

While we cannot heal all pain our students suffer, we can soften our students' distress with *positive* compassion—a smile, a hug, a comforting word, a helping hand, friendship. We can stop hurting hearts from breaking.

Emily Parker

"Miss Parker sounds like a social worker!" Gayle said.

"Miss Parker thinks she's a miracle worker," Laura said. "She believes *all* students can be stimulated to succeed."

"*All* students can be stimulated to succeed?" Tom guffawed.

"What a joke!" Sandy Turner sneered.

After school, Tracy, Stephen, Brittney, and Ricky sat in the corridor outside Miss Parker's classroom, waiting for Mrs. Nelson to exit.

Brittney looked up from the history book she was reading, and sighed. "My history class is so boring. English class is never boring."

"Miss Parker's class is never boring because we're always doing something *stimulating*," Tracy said, pleased with herself for using one of the vocabulary words she had learned in English class.

"Yeah, *stimulating* stuff!" Ricky said. "Like writing poems today about what road we want to take in life."

"And having class outside!" Brittney said. "Did you guys have class outside last Friday?"

"Yeah," Tracy, Stephen, and Ricky chorused.

"Did Miss Parker read that awesome quote about the sun to your classes?" Brittney said.

Tracy opened her English notebook and read aloud: "'...the sun shall shine more brightly than ever he has done, shall perchance shine into our minds and hearts, and light up our whole lives with a great awakening light.'"

"Henry David Thoreau," Stephen said.

Tracy smiled. "You're a bright student, Stephen Bernelli!"

Laura stood, arms crossed, in front of Emily's desk. "Compassion is not an academic objective."

"But it is a teaching objective," Emily said.

Laura frowned. "Your objective is supposed to be teaching your subject."

"My objective is supposed to be teaching students." Emily smiled.

POSITIVE TEACHERS
ARE PATIENT

CHAPTER 5

On the last Friday morning of the first quarter, a teacher workday/ student holiday, Leon Williams read the first year teachers' primary objective synopses that he had intended to review sooner. Emily Parker's positive teaching objectives aroused his attention. He pondered the stimulating power her teaching strategies reflected:

Positive Strategies

"Teachers open the door..."

—Chinese proverb

Objective: I will employ teaching strategies that stimulate students to learn.

1. *Energizing academic tedium* stimulates students to learn.

2. *Balancing telling with asking* stimulates students to learn.

3. *Including subjective questions on assignments* stimulates students to learn.

4. *Applying analogies* stimulates students to learn.

5. *Dismissing formality that compromises core objectives* stimulates students to learn.

6. *Incorporating creative activities* stimulates students to learn.

7. *Employing variant teaching modes* stimulates students to learn.

8. *Teaching effective study skills* stimulates students to learn.

9. *Promoting subject oriented supplementary reading* stimulates students to learn.

10. *Using positive evaluation methods* stimulates students to learn.

Emily Parker

Leon reviewed the first year teacher quarterly evaluations that Phil Malone, one of his assistant principals, had turned in the day before. Emily Parker was the only first year teacher with no negative scores or negative comments on her evaluation report.

"Tell me about your observation of Emily Parker," Leon spoke to Phil Malone later that morning. "I was surprised to see that a first year teacher had a perfect evaluation report."

"I found her teaching skills impeccable!" Phil said. "I've never seen a teacher quite like Emily Parker."

"How's that?" Leon said.

Phil smiled. "She's the epitome of a positive teacher."

Emily Parker's classroom reflected a cheerful ambiance of color—artwork posters on the walls, a pot of yellow mums on her desktop.

"Your positive teaching postures must make a notable difference in your freshmen students' academic performance," Leon said.

"All of my students have A/B averages," Emily said.

"*All* of your students?"

"Yes." Emily smiled.

"Miss Parker, I taught for fifteen years before I became a principal, and I never experienced *all* of my students succeeding simultaneously. How is it that a new teacher like yourself has stimulated a hundred and fifty freshmen—basic skills and general students—to achieve academic success?"

Emily pointed at the banner—All Eagles are supposed to soar!—above her chalkboard. "I believe *all* students are supposed to succeed, Mr. Williams."

How many teachers and administrators believe all students are sup-
posed to succeed? Leon contemplated as he went back to his office.
Most of us assume that some students will succeed, and some
won't—some students can succeed, and some can't.

Never have I heard any teacher or administrator say they believe all
students are supposed to succeed. Never have I known a teacher to stim-
ulate all of her students to succeed.

Leon spent all day Saturday in the guidance department, reviewing Emily Parker's students' cumulative academic records. A small
number of her students had maintained A/B averages throughout
their school years. A majority had sustained C status. Some had perpetually fluctuated between average and below average, and some
had failed particular classes. Several had failed a previous grade, and
several were repeating ninth grade.

Four of Emily Parker's students had failed two grades: Tracy
Daniels—failed first grade, repeating ninth; Stephen Bernelli—failed
third grade, repeating ninth; Brittney Anderson—failed second
grade, repeating ninth; Ricky Reinhardt—failed fifth grade, repeating ninth.

Maybe all of Miss Parker's students have A/B averages because she's
teaching below grade level…no, Phil Malone said that her lesson
seemed quite challenging for a basic skills English class. Maybe Mrs.
Nelson's mentoring is the positive influence.

Leon left the guidance department and walked down the hall to
his office. He sat down at his desk and read the tenured teacher quarterly evaluation reports that new assistant principal Carla Diega had
turned in. Laura Nelson's evaluation report, and many other tenured
teachers' evaluations, reflected negative scores and negative comments.

POSITIVE TEACHERS
ARE COMPASSIONATE

CHAPTER 6

❋

Monday morning Leon Williams called Tracy Daniels, Stephen Bernelli, Brittney Anderson, and Ricky Reinhardt to his office to speak with each of them one-on-one.

"Hi, Tracy. Please have a seat," Leon said.

"Am I in trouble?" Tracy asked.

"No, you're not in trouble. I just want to talk to you about your English grades this quarter."

"I have an A average! I usually make D's and F's in English."

"What's the difference this year?" Leon said.

"My teacher Miss Parker."

"How's Miss Parker making a difference for you, Tracy?"

"She helps me." Tracy smiled.

"Hi, Brittney. Please have a seat," Leon said.

"Have I done something wrong?" Brittney asked.

"No, you've done nothing wrong. I just want to talk to you about your English grades this quarter."

"I have a B average. I usually make D's and F's in English."

"What's the difference this year?" Leon said.

"My teacher Miss Parker."

"How's Miss Parker making a difference for you, Brittney?"

"She helps me." Brittney smiled.

"Hi, Stephen. Please have a seat," Leon said.

Stephen frowned. "I'm in trouble, right?"

"No, I just want to talk to you about your English grades this quarter."

"I have an A average! I usually make D's and F's in English."

"What's the difference this year?" Leon said.

"My teacher Miss Parker."

"How's Miss Parker making a difference for you, Stephen?"

"She helps me." Stephen smiled.

"Hi, Ricky. Please have a seat," Leon said.

"I know, you want to talk to me about being tardy twice last week. Well, my mom…"

"I want to talk to you about your English grades this quarter."

"I have a B average. I've never made a B in English or any other class!"

"What's the difference this year?" Leon said.

"My teacher Miss Parker."

"How's Miss Parker making a difference for you, Ricky?"

"She helps me." Ricky smiled.

"Thanks for coming in this afternoon, Mrs. Daniels," Leon said.

"Has Tracy been acting up at school?" Mrs. Daniels asked.

"Oh, no. She hasn't had any discipline referrals. I just wanted to meet you and talk to you about your daughter."

Mrs. Daniels smiled. "Tracy seems to be a different girl since school started."

"Different?" Leon said.

"Like night and day! When she failed last year, she said she was going to quit school when she turns sixteen. Now she's talking about what she wants to do after she graduates. Says she thinks she might want to be a first grade teacher."

"What do you think has stimulated the change in your daughter?"

"A teacher who cares about students. Miss Parker, Tracy's English teacher."

"Thanks for coming in this afternoon, Mr. Bernelli," Leon said.

"Did Stephen get in a fight?" Mr. Bernelli asked.

"No fights," Leon said. "I just wanted to meet you and talk to you about your son."

Mr. Bernelli smiled. "Stephen's really turned around this year."

"Turned around?" Leon said.

"Stephen's always hated school. But this year he says he likes it."

"What do you think has stimulated the change in your son?"

"A teacher who knows how to teach. Miss Parker, Stephen's English teacher."

"Thanks for coming in this afternoon, Mrs. Reinhardt," Leon said.

"If this is about Ricky being tardy, it was my fault," Mrs. Reinhardt said.

"It's not about Ricky being tardy. I just wanted to meet you and talk to you about your son."

"Ricky failed every class last year. But this year he's passing every class. Even has a B in English!" Mrs. Reinhardt smiled.

"What do you think has stimulated the change in your son?"

"A motivating teacher. Miss Parker, Ricky's English teacher."

"Thanks for coming in this afternoon, Mrs. Anderson," Leon said.

"I hope Brittney's not having behavioral problems," Mrs. Anderson said.

"No problems. I just wanted to meet you and talk to you about your granddaughter. I understand you're her legal guardian?"

"Yes, I am. I've raised Brittney since she was seven years old, since her parents died in a car accident."

"Before her parents died, Brittney was at the top of her first grade class, bright little girl. Then she just shut down in school after she lost her mom and dad. But this year she's finally bounced back. She's that bright girl again!" Mrs. Anderson smiled.

"What do you think has stimulated the change in your granddaughter?"

"A teacher who loves her students. Miss Parker, Brittney's English teacher."

POSITIVE TEACHERS
ENCOURAGE STUDENTS

CHAPTER 7

❀

Tuesday morning most of Laura Nelson's students wore somber expressions as they walked into class after receiving their first quarter grade reports in homeroom. Chad Bernelli's face was stormy; Julie Johnson's was wet with tears.

"Today is the beginning of the second quarter grading period," Laura said after the tardy bell rang. "I suggest you people get serious about your work in here if you want to pass the semester."

"If you don't pass this semester, you'll be lacking a half credit in senior English which means you'll not be graduating in June."

Emily Parker's second period students crowded around her desk, showing her their first quarter grade reports.

"I passed all of my subjects!" Eddie announced.

"So did I!" Samantha said.

"Me, too!" Melanie said.

"Me, too—me, too—me, too…"

"I made the A/B honor roll!" Tracy declared.

"Me, too," Nathan said.

"So did I!" Juan said.

"I did, too—I did, too—I did, too…"

Chad Bernelli stepped into Leon Williams' office during lunch period. "Excuse me, sir. I need to talk to you."

"Sure." Leon extended his hand to Heritage High's star quarterback.

"I need your help, Mr. Williams," Chad said, his expression taut. "I want to transfer to another senior English teacher, but guidance told me that I need your approval to transfer after the first quarter grading period."

"Why do you want to transfer, Chad?"

"I failed English this quarter. And I'm afraid I'll fail it for this semester; and then I won't graduate because I'll be lacking a half credit in senior English."

"Is this the first time you've ever failed an English class, Chad?"

"This is the first time I've ever failed any class!"

"Why do you think you failed English this quarter, Chad?"

"My teacher Mrs. Nelson. She doesn't explain anything, she doesn't review anything. If we ask questions, she cuts us down with rude remarks. She gives us homework every night and every weekend. A lot of teachers are like Mrs. Nelson, but Mrs. Nelson's the worst of the worst, Mr. Williams."

Leon picked up his phone and called the guidance director: "How many students failed Mrs. Nelson's English classes first quarter?"

Laura Nelson charged into Leon's office after school. "Why did you approve a transfer for Chad Bernelli?"

"Chad was concerned he might fail the semester which would prevent him from graduating in June," Leon said.

"Chad Bernelli failed my class first quarter because he's too wrapped up in football. A different teacher won't change that!"

"Mrs. Nelson, Chad's been playing football since his freshman year. He's never failed a class before."

"Thirty-five percent of your students failed your class first quarter. That's a high percentage, Mrs. Nelson."

"It's a normal percentage for the first quarter, Mr. Williams."

"A thirty-five percent failure rate is normal? Miss Parker had *no* failures for the first quarter. In fact, all of her students made A's and B's."

"All A's and B's? I'd question her academic standards if I were you, Mr. Williams!"

"I intend to thoroughly scrutinize Miss Parker's teaching success. You're dismissed from support teacher duty, Mrs. Nelson; I'll confer with Miss Parker myself. I'll have my secretary put a memo in her faculty box, notifying her of the change."

"Fine with me, Mr. Williams!"

At four o'clock Leon picked up his briefcase, walked out of his office, and headed out to the parking lot in front of the school.

"Mr. Williams, have you got a minute?" Greg King, head football coach, a muscular middle-aged man, jogged up beside him.

"Sure, Coach."

"Chad Bernelli told me that he talked to you about why he failed English first quarter. Said he asked for a transfer and you approved it. Well, I have three other players who failed a class first quarter, and they have the same story about their teachers."

"Coach, I can't transfer every student who failed a class first quarter," Leon said.

"I realize that, Mr. Williams. What I wanted to talk to you about was school policy dictating that extracurricular sports participants who fail a class aren't eligible to continue playing. I don't want to put these four boys off the football team because I know for a fact that none of them are academic goof-offs."

Leon took a notepad and pen out of his shirt pocket. "Who are the other three players who failed a class?"

"Senior Manuel Garcia, junior Jesse Collins, and sophomore Tony Weaver."

"Coach, I'll look into this and get back to you by the end of the day Friday. In the meantime, your four players who failed a class stay on the team."

Greg smiled, "Thanks, Mr. Williams."

"Working overtime, Miss Parker?" Leon commented as Emily Parker approached them.

"Coach's hours, huh?" Greg laughed. "Speaking of coach's hours, I better get back to my team!" He tipped his red cap at Emily, and jogged off toward the football field.

"What keeps you so late today, Miss Parker?" Leon said.

"My success class ran longer than normal," she said.

"Success class?" Leon said.

"After school tutorial for my critically challenged students. Success class sounds more enticing than tutorial." She smiled.

"How many students attend your success class?"

"I have four students who attend every day. Others come in as they need special help."

"Bet I can guess the names of the four students who attend every day." Leon grinned. "Tracy Daniels, Stephen Bernelli, Brittney Anderson, and Ricky Reinhardt. Am I right?"

"How did you guess?" Emily said.

Leon winked. "Principal's intuition. But what I don't know is how you influence critically challenged students to attend an elective tutorial every day after school. It's been my observation that most challenged students dislike school, period. I agree that calling your tutorial a success class is an enticing stimulus, but what's your main stimulus?"

Emily smiled. "I give them positive hope. I help them believe they can succeed."

POSITIVE TEACHERS
REFLECT
POSITIVE ATTITUDES

CHAPTER 8

❁

Wednesday morning Leon commenced one-on-one interviews with students who had failed Laura Nelson's English classes first quarter.

"Tim, you failed English this past quarter?"

"Yes, sir, I did," Tim Barber, a tall, lanky senior, answered.

"Have you ever failed an English class before?"

"No, sir, I haven't."

"Why did you fail this past quarter?"

"My teacher Mrs. Nelson."

"How did you fail because of your teacher?" Leon said.

"Mrs. Nelson doesn't explain anything," Tim said.

"Lucas, you failed English this past quarter?"

"Yes, sir, I did," Lucas Medina, a stocky senior, answered.

"Have you ever failed an English class before?"

"Yes, sir, I have."

"When?" Leon asked.

"Eighth grade. When I had a teacher like Mrs. Nelson."

"Like Mrs. Nelson?"

"A teacher who doesn't explain anything," Lucas said.

"Julie, you failed English this past quarter?"

"Yes, sir, I did," Julie Johnson answered.

"Have you ever failed an English class before?"

"No, sir, I haven't. I've never done very good in English—I mean very well—but I've never failed."

"Why did you fail English this past quarter?"

Tears welled in Julie's eyes. "Because...because Mrs. Nelson doesn't explain anything."

By noon Friday Leon had concluded interviews with the fifty-two students who had failed Laura Nelson's senior English classes first quarter. All fifty-two students named Laura Nelson as the primary reason they had failed.

After lunch period Leon interviewed the other football players who had failed a subject first quarter.

"You failed Algebra II first quarter, is that correct?" Leon asked fullback Tony Weaver.

"Yes, sir, I did," Tony said.

"Have you ever failed a math class before?"

"Algebra I, last year," Tony answered.

"Why did you fail Algebra I, Tony?"

"I didn't understand it. But I passed it in summer school."

"You didn't understand Algebra I last year, but you understood Algebra I this summer?"

"Different teacher this summer," Tony said.

"Who was your Algebra teacher last year?"

"Mr. Edwards, same teacher I have this year," Tony said.

"You failed American history first quarter, is that correct?" Leon asked halfback Jesse Collins.

"Yes, sir, I did," Jesse said.

"Have you ever failed a history class before?"

"No, sir, I haven't," Jesse answered.

"Why did you fail American history, Jesse?"

"Mrs. Turner doesn't explain anything. Just gives us reading assignments and worksheets."

"You failed ecology first quarter, is that correct?" Leon asked linebacker Manuel Garcia.

"Yes, sir, I did," Manuel said.

"Have you ever failed a science class before?"

"Biology, ninth grade," Manuel answered. "But I passed biology when I repeated it in tenth grade."

"What changed between failing biology in ninth grade and passing biology the following year?"

"The teacher," Manuel said.

"So the teacher makes the difference between failing or passing a subject, Manuel?"

"A teacher who teaches makes the difference, Mr. Williams."

"I'd like to talk to you about one of your students who failed your Algebra II class first quarter—Tony, second period," Leon spoke to Tom Edwards after school.

"Tony doesn't apply himself. He didn't last year, and he isn't this year," Tom said.

"But Tony applied himself in summer school. He repeated Algebra I and passed," Leon said.

"He wasn't involved in sports during summer school session."

"So sports participation is the reason Tony failed Algebra I last year and Algebra II first quarter this semester, Mr. Edwards?"

"That's the main reason, yes."

"Thirty-one percent of your students failed your algebra classes first quarter, Mr. Edwards. Do all of those students participate in sports?"

"Mrs. Turner, I'd like to talk to you about one of your students who failed your American history class first quarter—Jesse, fourth period."

"Jesse failed almost every test last nine weeks," Sandy Turner said.

"Jesse has never failed a history class before, Mrs. Turner."

"Maybe American history is more difficult for him to learn."

"Thirty-four percent of your students failed American history first quarter, Mrs. Turner. Is American history so difficult to learn that forty-seven students didn't pass?"

"Mrs. Stone, I'd like to talk to you about one of your students who failed your ecology class first quarter—Manuel, fifth period."

"Manuel seems to lack aptitude for science, like so many students," Gayle Stone said.

"Like thirty percent of your students, Mrs. Stone? The thirty percent who failed your class?"

Leon left his office at three-thirty and walked out to the P.E. field where Coach King's varsity football players were practicing. A chilly breeze blew across the field, scattering errant autumn leaves.

"Coach, I interviewed all of the students who failed Laura Nelson's English classes, the class that Chad failed. And I interviewed Tony, Jesse, and Manuel, and the teachers of the classes they failed." Leon smiled. "Coach, your boys have my permission to continue playing second quarter."

POSITIVE TEACHERS
PRAISE STUDENTS

CHAPTER 9

❁

Thursday morning Leon observed Emily Parker's second, third, and fourth period freshmen English classes. "If I didn't know differently, I'd assume your basic skills and general students were honor students. They're all so bright and responsive," Leon said after Emily's fourth period students left for lunch hour.

"*All* students are potentially bright, Mr. Williams."

"You're on a teaching mission, aren't you?" Leon said.

Emily smiled. "Yes."

"I'm curious to know what inspired your mission, Miss Parker."

"My brother Todd." Emily picked up the framed photo of her brother and handed it to Leon.

"Handsome boy," he said.

"A challenged student." Emily's eyes filled with tears. "My brother committed suicide because of the chronic distress he suffered as a challenged student. He was labeled academically challenged in the first grade. Every school year the threat of failure pursued him, and then the threat became reality when he failed fifth grade and had to repeat. Four years later, he failed ninth grade. The day before Todd was to commence repeating ninth grade, he loaded our father's pistol, put it to his head, and pulled the trigger."

"Positive teachers could have facilitated a different destiny for my brother. Regardless of his learning disabilities, positive teachers could have stimulated him to succeed."

"No special academic help was offered to your brother? Classes or programs for challenged students?"

"Oh yes. But special classes and special programs don't stimulate students to succeed, Mr. Williams; positive teachers stimulate students to succeed."

At four o'clock rain poured from a lightning charged sky. Julie stood under the portico at the front of the school. "Waiting for a ride?" Leon asked as he stepped outside and opened his umbrella.

"I'm waiting for the rain to stop so I can walk home," Julie answered.

"Might not stop for a while. I can take you home, Julie. Where do you live?"

"North Tenth Street." Julie smiled. "Thanks, Mr. Williams." Leon shared his umbrella with Julie and they dashed to his car.

"What kept you after school today?" Leon asked as he drove out of the parking lot.

"I was working on an art project," Julie said. "I'm drawing a pen and ink sketch of my brother—extra credit points, I hope, for a paper we have to write for English."

"What kind of paper are you writing?"

"A profile of a remarkable person. It's a required paper in all senior English classes. Mrs. Nelson said it will be twenty-five percent of our second quarter grade in her classes."

"Who are you going to write about, Julie?"

"My brother Timothy." Julie brushed tears from her eyes. "Timothy died of heart failure this past summer. Sometimes I miss him so much, I think I'm going to lose my mind. Schoolwork's been hard for me this semester. I don't understand a lot of what I read, and I forget things."

"It's difficult to concentrate when we're distressed, Julie. I learned that fact from a very positive lady, a new English teacher at Heritage."

"Miss Parker?" Julie said.

"You know Miss Parker?"

"My neighbor Tracy told me about her. Miss Parker's her English teacher. Tracy made an A in English first quarter which is a miracle for her because she failed English last year."

"Tracy said everyone in her English class has A/B averages. And she said the class isn't easy, but Miss Parker helps them learn. And she makes it fun and interesting, not boring like most classes. She teaches them all kinds of success stuff, too."

Julie smiled. "If *all* teachers were like Miss Parker, *no one* would fail!"

"She teaches them all kinds of success stuff," Julie's comment echoed in Leon's thoughts that evening as he read Emily Parker's fifth synopsis:

Positive Empowerment

"Do the thing and you'll have the power."

—Ralph Waldo Emerson

Objective: I will teach my students goal structuring skills which facilitate academic success.

Positive purposes for learning academic goal structuring skills:

A. Goals can take you where you want to go.
B. Goals reduce the work involved in achieving an objective.
C. Goals let you know if you have succeeded.

Positive guidelines for academic goal structuring:

A. Your goals should be written and stated in an affirmative form.
B. Your goals should be specific.
C. Your goals should be realistic and attainable, but challenging.
D. Your goals should be measurable.
E. Identify where you are in relation to your goals.
F. Define the activities that lead to reaching your goals.
G. What do you need to "become" to achieve your goals?
H. What, if any, supplies, equipment, or situations do you need to attain your goals?

Emily Parker

All teachers should teach academic goal structuring skills—what a difference it would make, Leon thought. *Such a difference it's made for all of Emily Parker's students.*

Julie Johnson's statement—*"If all teachers were like Miss Parker, no one would fail!"* saturated Leon's spirit.

POSITIVE TEACHERS
ARE ENTHUSIASTIC

CHAPTER 10

❀

"**I** called this special meeting to address a serious issue," Leon spoke to the faculty Friday afternoon. "We have almost fifteen hundred students here at Heritage High. Twenty percent of these students failed one or more classes first quarter. This means three hundred students did not pass one or more classes."

"I believe all of us can calculate twenty percent of fifteen hundred, Mr. Williams," Tom Edwards snapped.

"Can all of your algebra students calculate percentages, Mr. Edwards?" Leon said.

"Of course they can't! Some of them still haven't learned multiplication tables. A lot of the students who didn't pass algebra first quarter are students who are deficient in basic math skills."

"So perhaps a comprehensive review of basic math skills would help?" Leon said.

Tom scowled. "Comprehensive review? They should have learned basic math in elementary and middle school!"

"You're right, Mr. Edwards. They should have learned basic math skills in elementary and middle school. But you're telling me they didn't."

"I think the rest of the faculty would agree with me that we don't have time to review what these kids should have learned and cover the subject curriculum we're supposed to, Mr. Williams."

"I agree!" Laura Nelson said.

"So do I—so do I—so do I!" several teachers concurred.

"Covering subject curriculum can't be the primary teaching objective if your students are deficient in particular basic skills and knowledge that they need to comprehend the curriculum you're teaching," Leon said.

"If subject curriculum isn't the primary teaching objective, then what is, Mr. Williams?" Gayle Stone frowned.

"Stimulating students to succeed, Mrs. Stone." Leon smiled.

"Comprehensive reviews are not going to stimulate some of these students who are just simply lazy, Mr. Williams," Sandy Turner said.

"Lazy, or unstimulated, Mrs. Turner?"

"Is there a difference?" Sandy rolled her eyes.

"Perhaps the teacher?" Leon said. "Indolence is a symptom of a core problem. Boredom is often the core problem."

"We're not here to entertain students, Mr. Williams," Laura said.

"No, you're not here to entertain students, Mrs. Nelson. You're here to teach students."

Jackie Adams, a new teacher, raised her hand. "Mr. Williams, I review every day, over and over and over again. But so many of my special ed students don't comprehend the most basic concepts. I think some of them are too critically challenged to succeed."

"I understand your perception, Miss Adams. But there was a young girl named Helen Keller who was blind and deaf and mute since babyhood, and a *positive* teacher—a patient, persistent, persevering teacher named Anne Sullivan—stimulated her to read and write and speak."

"Our new English teacher Emily Parker wrote a profound synopsis—'Positive Conviction.' I'd like each of you to read her synopsis." Leon handed assistant principal Carla Diega a stack of papers. "Mrs. Diega, would you please give everyone a copy."

"You're asking those of us who are experienced and tenured to read something written by a new teacher?" Tom Edwards spoke out. "How much could a new teacher know about teaching?"

"Obviously Emily Parker knows a great deal," Leon answered. "*None* of her students failed first quarter."

"Where is Miss Parker?" Laura Nelson said, glancing around the library conference room.

"Miss Parker is conducting her after school 'success class' for critically challenged students," Leon said.

"That excuses her from attending a faculty meeting?" Laura said.

"Mrs. Nelson, I'll excuse anyone who is working after school to stimulate students to succeed."

"I've been teaching at Heritage for twenty years. Never has a principal excused teachers from attending faculty meetings," Laura said. "And never has a Heritage principal questioned the teaching competency of tenured faculty!"

Greg King stood. "Maybe it's time someone did, Mrs. Nelson! I help my football players with homework assignments after practice, and I've certainly questioned the academic value of some of the assignments I've seen."

"And what would you know about academic assignments, Coach King? You're a P.E. teacher!"

"I know that copying every dictionary definition listed for twenty vocabulary words each week is not conducive to positive learning, Mrs. Nelson."

"Positive learning? What are you teaching your football players, allowing them to continue playing when they failed a subject first semester? You're teaching them that it's okay to fail a class. And you're in violation of school academic standards, Coach King!"

"I gave Coach King permission to allow his players who failed a subject first quarter to continue participating," Leon said.

"You gave him permission to violate school academic standards?" Laura said.

"Yes, I did, because initially I had reason to believe there could be valid cause those students failed a subject first quarter. And after investigation, I'm convinced there was."

"What valid cause?" Laura fumed.

"Negative teaching, Mrs. Nelson—the core reason, I believe, that twenty percent of our students failed one or more classes first quarter. The reason we'll continue meeting once a week this second quarter—to discuss positive teaching postures that stimulate students to succeed."

POSITIVE TEACHERS PERSEVERE

CHAPTER 11

❁

"I hope Mr. Williams is off his high horse this week," Gayle Stone said to Sandy Turner as they walked through the library doors the next Friday afternoon.

"I wouldn't count on it." Sandy pointed to a banner—All Eagles are supposed to soar!—strung across the end of the conference room where Leon stood behind a lectern.

"The topic for today's meeting is Positive Strategies," Leon announced after the teachers were seated.

"Emily Parker's positive strategies, I see." Tom Edwards held up the handout everyone had received.

"A positive teacher's strategies." Leon smiled.

"Energizing academic tedium stimulates students to learn," Leon said, referring to the first strategy listed on the handout.

"What's your operational definition of academic tedium?" Chuck Canton, the new agriculture teacher, queried.

"Positive question, Mr. Canton! Academic tedium is academic material that doesn't stimulate students to learn—tedious textbooks, tedious worksheets, tedious assignments and exercises," he explained.

"Are you suggesting we throw away our textbooks and all of our teaching materials, Mr. Williams?" Laura Nelson sneered.

"I'm suggesting you energize your textbooks and teaching materials, Mrs. Nelson." Leon smiled.

"Balancing telling and asking stimulates students to learn," Leon said in reference to the second strategy listed on the handout. "Why would balancing telling and asking stimulate students to learn?" he asked.

"Students might pay more attention to the lesson if they thought they might be asked a question!" junior English teacher Pamela Owens laughed.

"Good point, Mrs. Owens!" Leon said.

"Too much telling—lecturing—can anesthetize students' attention to the lesson," American government teacher Bill Schartz said.

"Another good point! Thank you, Mr. Schartz."

"Asking induces active participation," world history teacher Mike Zantini said.

"Yes! Thank you, Mr. Zantini."

"Including subjective questions on assignments stimulates students to learn," Leon said. "Too often assignment questions are objective which doesn't stimulate what?" he asked.

"Critical thinking," sophomore English teacher Jeff Young answered.

"Correct, Mr. Young!" Leon said.

"What kind of subjective questions can be asked about algebra?" Tom Edwards scowled.

"You could ask your students why they enjoy studying algebra," Leon said.

Tom frowned. "They don't enjoy studying algebra."

"Then ask them why." Leon smiled.

"Applying analogies stimulates students to learn," Leon said.

"Mrs. Nelson, what analogy might you apply to the purpose of parts of speech?"

"Parts of speech are parts of speech, Mr. Williams," Laura snapped.

"Parts of speech are like parts of an engine," Jeff Young said. "Each part has a particular function."

"Excellent analogy, Mr. Young!"

"Dismissing formality that compromises core objectives stimulates students to learn," Leon said.

"And what's that supposed to mean?" Gayle Stone said.

"Who can tell us what it means?" Leon said.

"I know!" freshmen English teacher Roberta Charles waved her hand. "It means eliminating tedious methods that aren't necessary to learn a particular skill; for example, formal outlining. Many of my students get confused about where the Roman numerals are placed, where the Arabic numbers are placed—the capital letters, the lower case letters—numbers in parentheses, letters in parentheses. So I teach them the formal outline structure, but I don't demand they use it if it compromises the core objective which is simply organizing topics."

"So what outlining format do your students use?" Gayle Stone glared at Roberta Charles.

"Whatever format works for them." Roberta smiled.

"Incorporating creative activities stimulates students to learn," Leon said. "Creative activities induce comprehension and critical thinking."

"For some of you—Mrs. Goldberg and Mrs. Allen, home economics; Mr. Dixon, woodworking; Mrs. Kline and Mr. Vanus, art—creative activities are an integral part of your curriculum."

"For those of you who teach academic subjects, what types of creative activities might be incorporated into your curriculum?"

"Subject oriented scrapbooks," Spanish teacher Maria Gonzales said. "My students love making scrapbooks about Spanish culture."

"Scrapbooks—great idea, Mrs. Gonzales!"

"Subject oriented picture puzzles," senior English teach Ellen Baker said. "Since senior English focuses on British literature, my students put together picture puzzles of English, Scottish, and Welsh architecture and landscapes."

"Picture puzzles—another great idea, Mrs. Baker!"

"Balancing teaching modes stimulates students to learn," Leon said. "Some students have learning mode preferences; in other words, a particular learning mode facilitates greater comprehension. For example, learning success for students who are preferentially auditory learners will be compromised if they are perpetually subjected to visual learning modes. Learning success for students who are preferentially visual learners will be compromised if they are perpetually subjected to auditory learning modes. The same principle applies to kinesthetic learners."

"Are you suggesting we compromise traditional teaching modes with time consuming kinetic learning activities?" Laura Nelson said.

Leon smiled. "I'm suggesting you stimulate your students to learn, Mrs. Nelson."

"Teaching effective study skills stimulates students to learn," Leon said. "When I was in school, our teachers told us to study, but they didn't teach us how to study for tests or how to review subject material."

"Were any of you taught how to study?" No one responded.

"Do any of you teach your students how to study?" No one responded.

"I taught history for fifteen years, and I'm sorry to say I didn't teach my students study skills," Leon said. "But it's been brought to my attention that learning effective study skills facilitates academic success, so I'm soliciting a stimulating video on the subject of learning effective study skills. You can pick one up on your way out today." He pointed to a stack of videos on a library table.

Guidance counselor Lisa Queen stood. "Mr. Williams, on the subject of studying, I have a concern. Most of our students have little time to study for tests or review subject material because they're inundated with a surfeit of daily homework assignments."

"Daily homework is a part of the academic discipline, Miss Queen!" geometry teacher Richard Chin spoke out. "Daily homework helps students learn."

"Twenty-four percent of your students failed your classes first quarter, Mr. Chin. I don't believe daily homework is stimulating all of your students to learn geometry!"

"Thank you, Miss Queen, for questioning the academic value of daily homework assignments," Leon interjected. He glanced at his watch. "We'll continue our survey of positive teaching strategies next week, Wednesday afternoon."

Laura Nelson tossed the handout in a wastebasket as she and Tom Edwards walked out of the library. "Leon Williams is a patronizing personality," Laura said.

"Yeah, he's an arrogant sort. Reminds me of a holier-than-thou preacher." Tom frowned.

"Well, he can preach positive teaching all he wants, but he's not converting me," Laura said.

Positive Teachers
Motivate Students

CHAPTER 12

"**P**romoting subject oriented supplementary reading stimulates students to learn," Leon opened the faculty meeting the last Wednesday afternoon of November, the day before Thanksgiving break.

"What kind of supplementary reading would be oriented to algebra?" Tom Edwards said.

"A biography of Albert Einstein?" Leon said.

"How would reading a biography of Albert Einstein stimulate my students to learn algebra?"

"Learning about a man whose passion was algebra might influence your students to develop a passion for algebra, Mr. Edwards."

Social studies teacher Jean McBrier frowned. "Who could be passionate about algebra?"

"I am!" Tom glared at Mrs. McBrier.

"Using positive evaluation methods stimulates students to learn," Leon said. He wrote *+50* on one poster board and *-50* on another poster board, and held up both so all the teachers could see them.

"Mr. Finch," he addressed the chemistry teacher. "What's the first thought that comes to your mind when you look at these grades?"

"*Plus fifty* looks like a better grade than *minus fifty*," Carl Finch said.

"What is it about *plus fifty* that looks like a better grade than *minus fifty* when in reality, they're both the same grade?"

"The plus sign symbolizes a positive connotation," Carl answered. "The minus sign symbolizes a negative connotation."

"Excellent analysis, Mr. Finch!"

"What are some other positive evaluation methods that reflect success instead of failure?" Leon asked.

"Not using a red ink pen to grade papers," home economics teacher Marilyn Allen said. "Red reflects a negative connotation."

"Writing positive comments on students' assignments and tests," art teacher Denise Kline said. "Finding something to praise."

"And what if there's nothing to praise?" Laura Nelson's voice reverberated sarcasm.

Denise smiled. "Well, you can always write a motivational comment."

"Last week we discussed the value of teaching positive study skills. How many of you have watched the study skills video?" Leon asked. Several teachers raised their hands.

"How many of you have shown the video to your students?" Mike Zantini, Pamela Owens, and Richard Chin raised their hands.

"Mr. Zantini, what significant effect has the study skills video generated in your history students' academic performance?" Leon said.

"My students watched the study skills video on Monday. Comparing their test scores last week to their scores today, my students' scores rose an average of ten percent."

Laura Nelson frowned. "That's significant?"

"It's especially significant to all of the students who passed this week's test after failing last week's!" Mike Zantini smiled.

"Mrs. Owens, what significant effect has the study skills video generated in your junior English students' academic performance?" Leon asked.

"Prior to watching the video, fifteen percent of my students perpetually failed the weekly vocabulary test. This week, however, all of my students passed."

"*All* of your students, Mrs. Owens?" Gayle Stone smirked.

"*All* of my students, Mrs. Stone." Pamela Owens smiled.

"And Mr. Chin, what significant effect has the study skills video generated in your geometry students' academic performance?" Leon asked.

Richard Chin smiled. "All of my students made A's and B's on their weekly test today."

In twenty-five years of teaching together at Heritage, Tom Edwards had never seen Richard Chin smile. Richard had always been a stern faced, hard-nosed, pedantic teacher personality. Like me, Tom thought.

"That Leon Williams really gets under my skin," Laura Nelson huffed as she and Tom Edwards left the library at three-thirty. "He and Emily Parker are a preposterous pair of idealists!" she ranted.

"None of Emily Parker's students failed first quarter, Laura."

"Tom, are you siding with those two positive teaching proselytes?"

"Well, to be truthful, I could put forth more effort. Maybe *all* students can be stimulated to succeed." He smiled.

"Really, Tom? Michael can't be stimulated to succeed!"

"But Michael's mentally retarded," he said.

Tears of anger stung Laura's eyes as she stomped away from Tom. "*Down's syndrome is a congenital condition characterized by moderate to severe mental retardation,*" the pediatrician's words from the past hit her hard as they had every day for sixteen years.

Tom walked down the corridor, his thoughts immersed in the past. Twenty years ago newlywed Laura Nelson had been a pert teacher fresh out of college—a whirlwind of energy and enthusiasm. She had been a dedicated teacher who worked before school, after school, and attended every extracurricular function. Her first year at Heritage, she was chosen Eagle Teacher of the Year.

When Laura had become pregnant, she told everyone that she had an Eagle "in the nest." "If it's a boy, he's going to be a Heritage football player one day—if it's a girl, she's going to be a Heritage cheerleader!" Laura had taken early maternity leave in the spring, excited about the little Eagle that she would be bringing to the football games in the fall. But Laura had never attended another Heritage football game after Michael was born. Laura had returned to school a different person. Life had dealt her a hard blow, dashing her dreams and suffocating her positive spirit.

"Tom, are you siding with those two positive teaching proselytes?" Laura's words rang in his thoughts. She wouldn't have understood if he had told her that seeing stern faced, hard-nosed, pedantic Richard Chin smile about his students' success had stimulated a change of heart. She wouldn't have understood that in a fraction of a moment, her colleague Tom Edwards—negative teacher for twenty-five years—had been converted to the positive side.

Sophomore fullback Tony Weaver was sitting on the steps in front of the school when Tom walked outside. "Hi, Tony," Tom spoke to his second period Algebra II student.

"Hi, Mr. Edwards."

"Have a great Thanksgiving break!" Tom smiled.

"You, too, Mr. Edwards." Tony smiled.

POSITIVE TEACHERS
TEACH
SUCCESS STRATEGIES

CHAPTER 13

"The topic for today's meeting is Positive Empowerment," Leon addressed the faculty the first Wednesday of December.

"Our primary job as educators is to empower our students to succeed—to incorporate into our academic curriculum the teaching of skills that will facilitate academic success. One of the most empowering success skills you can teach your students is academic goal structuring," Leon said.

"That sounds like a job for guidance counselors!" Latin teacher Barbara Lanier spoke out.

"Mrs. Lanier, empowering your students to succeed in your class is your job," Leon responded.

"Positive purposes for learning academic goal structuring skills," Leon read Emily Parker's synopsis of which every teacher had received a copy. "Goals can take you where you want to go. Goals reduce the work involved in achieving an objective. Goals let you know if you have succeeded."

"Why is it important to first communicate to your students the purposes for goal structuring?" Leon asked.

"To stimulate them to set goals," health teacher Michelle Hunter said.

"Yes, Mrs. Hunter! If we don't have a purpose for doing something, we have no stimulation to do it. You can teach positive health

habits all day long, but your students will not be stimulated to practice positive health habits unless you give them a purpose for practicing positive health habits. Am I right, Mrs. Hunter?"

"Absolutely!" Michelle agreed.

"How do you stimulate teenagers to practice positive health habits, Mrs. Hunter?" Laura Nelson frowned. "Most of them exist on a
pizza diet, and their main exercise is pushing remote control buttons
or clicking a computer mouse!"

"I stimulate my female students to practice positive health habits
by emphasizing proper nutrition and exercise as the most effective
beauty aids. I stimulate my male students to practice positive health
habits by emphasizing proper nutrition and exercise as the main elements of building and maintaining a strong physique. And I stimulate both female and male students to practice positive health habits
by emphasizing proper nutrition and exercise as brain energizers
that affect better academic performance."

"What stimulating purpose do you give your students for learning
grammar, literature, and composition, Mrs. Nelson?" Leon asked.

Laura glared at Leon. "Passing and graduating."

"And that's what, about sixty-five percent effective in your English
classes, Mrs. Nelson?"

"Are you trying your best to be condescending, Mr. Williams?"

"I'm *trying* my best to wake you up, Mrs. Nelson."

"Now let's discuss the positive guidelines for academic goal structuring," Leon said.

"Goals should be written and stated in an affirmative form. Why
is this important?"

"Written goals facilitate commitment. Verbal goals are easily
ignored or forgotten," Bill Schartz said.

"And how would you define *affirmative form*, Mr. Schartz?"

"Saying *I will* instead of *I want to* or *I'll try to.*"
"Excellent definition of *affirmative form*, Mr. Schartz!"

"Goals should be specific. Why do academic goals need to be specific?" Leon asked.

"Because non-specific goals don't stimulate success," business education teacher Cheryl Azelski said.

"Would you please give us an example, Mrs. Azelski."

"I see it every year at the beginning of school. Students come in the first day, stimulated with the energy of a fresh start: 'I'm going to do better this year!' Within a week, though, they're the same students they were the year before because they didn't structure specific goals to become a better student," Cheryl said.

"Thank you, Mrs. Azelski."

"Goals should be realistic and attainable, but challenging. Mr. Finch, how would you define this guideline for structuring academic goals?" Leon asked.

"Realistic and attainable academic goals are incremental goals that facilitate measurable success in manageable steps," Carl said.

"Thank you, Mr. Finch, for explaining the framework of realistic and attainable, but challenging academic goals."

"Goals should be measurable, as Mr. Finch just implied. If there's no standard for measuring success, success has no definitive denotation."

"In other words, the academic goal *I will be a better student* has no meaning if *better* isn't qualified with a standard of success measurement," Cheryl Azelski said.

"Exactly, Mrs. Azelski. Thank you."

"When you teach academic goal structuring, ask your students to identify where they are in relation to their goals. Why is this step important? Mrs. Gonzales?" Leon asked.

"Identifying where they are in relation to their goals provides a sense of reality and a sense of necessary direction for achieving their goals," Maria said.

"Very good! Thank you, Mrs. Gonzales."

"Define the activities that lead to reaching specific goals. This is the most significant element of goal structuring," Leon said.

"Say a student's goal is to improve his or her algebra average a letter grade. To achieve that goal, the student must define the specific activities that will facilitate reaching that goal. *Study more* must be defined as *study thirty minutes every night*, for example."

"Many, if not most, students lack proficiency in identifying specific activities that are necessary to achieve their goals. They'll need your help with this step."

"The seventh step—What do you need to become to achieve specific goals?—stimulates students to consider what postures facilitate goal success," Leon said. "Mr. Vanus, what postures would you stress as imperative to achieving goals?"

"I'd stress self-discipline, time management, personal organization, and positive thinking," art teacher David Vanus said.

"Positive thinking?" Leon said.

"An *I can do it* attitude," David replied.

"Excellent! Thank you, Mr. Vanus."

"The last goal structuring step—What, if any, supplies, equipment, or situations are needed to attain specific goals?—is a crucial step for goal achievement," Leon said.

"Help your students determine what they need to actualize their goals, and help them find the resources that will provide those elements essential to their success. Of course, what your students need *more than anything* is your support." Leon smiled.

Tom caught up with Laura as she walked to the parking lot after the faculty meeting. "I'm sorry I upset you last week. I understand why you don't want to be the teacher you used to be."

"And what's that supposed to mean?" Laura scowled.

"Before Michael was born, you were a dynamic teacher—like Emily Parker. I resented your positive teaching energy because I was such a miserable teacher. I loved algebra, but I didn't like teaching."

"But you've had a change of heart, haven't you?" Laura glared at him.

"Yes." Tom smiled.

"Well, I haven't, Edwards!"

POSITIVE TEACHERS
ARE ATTENTIVE

CHAPTER 14

The second Wednesday morning of December, Leon reviewed Emily Parker's sixth synopsis:

Positive Communication

"Let no corrupt communication proceed out of your mouth, but that which is good to the use of edifying…"

—Ephesians 4:29

Objective: I will communicate positive messages that encourage and empower my students.

Students need inspiration and hope. They need teachers who convey positive messages that motivate them to learn and succeed—teachers who impart optimism that they can succeed.

What we say to our students, and how we say it, is relative to our students' academic success potential. Communicate positive statements and positive responses are stimulated. Communicate negative statements and negative responses are stimulated. *All* students are motivated by positive statements. *No* students are motivated by negative statements. The significance of positive infusion versus negative infusion is the profound disparity between students soaring and students failing.

Emily Parker

"Our topics today are Positive Compassion and Positive Communication," Leon addressed the faculty Wednesday afternoon.

"Positive compassion? Are we teachers or ministers, Mr. Williams?" Gayle Stone frowned.

"In my experience teaching, Mrs. Stone, I ministered to students in just about every capacity imaginable—surrogate dad, coach, confidante, counselor," Leon said. "Positive compassion is a willingness to minister to students via whatever auxiliary role or action might solve or alleviate personal distress that interferes with students' ability to learn."

"Expecting students to concentrate on academic instruction when they're focused on personal distress is an unrealistic expectation," Leon read Emily's synopsis.

"A student who is sick cannot concentrate on learning and succeeding. A student who suffers from abuse, neglect, or deprivation, cannot concentrate on learning and succeeding. A student who is hungry for food, or love, or acceptance, cannot concentrate on learning and succeeding."

"Teachers, neither you nor I can heal all personal pain our students suffer, but with positive compassion—a smile, a hug, a comforting word, a helping hand, friendship—we can soften our students' distress. We can stop hurting hearts from breaking."

"Stop hurting hearts from breaking?" Laura Nelson sneered.

"Yes, Mrs. Nelson," Leon replied. "Like your student Julie Johnson. Her brother died this past summer. Julie's hurting; she needs positive compassion."

"Julie Johnson's my student, too," business math teacher Nancy McIntosh said. "I wasn't aware that she lost her brother this past summer. How are we supposed to know what our students are suffering?"

"We need to ask, Mrs. McIntosh," Leon said. "When we notice a student seems depressed, or out of sorts, we need to ask: Are you sick? Are you worried about something? You seem sad, you seem upset—what's wrong?"

"The basis of many students' personal distress is academic despair. We need to convey positive messages that motivate students to learn and succeed. We need to impart optimism that they can succeed," Leon said.

"What we say to our students, and how we say it, is relative to our students' academic success potential. Communicate positive statements and positive responses are stimulated. Communicate negative statements and negative responses are stimulated. *All* students are motivated by positive statements. *No* students are motivated by negative statements. The significance of positive infusion versus negative infusion is the profound disparity between students soaring and students failing."

"Positive communication can save lives," Derrick Jordan, Heritage High's resident police officer, interjected. "Suicides are often stimulated by the proverbial 'hair that broke the camel's back.' A student who is not succeeding academically, and suffers other problems as well, comes to school in a state of dangerous distress. A teacher's negative words can provoke a student to break."

"Officer Jordan, are you suggesting teachers always use positive language, no matter the situation?" Laura Nelson scoffed.

"I'm imploring you to always use positive language, no matter the situation," he answered.

"Well, I don't intend to pamper unruly, lazy kids with positive euphemisms," she snorted.

"Positive language isn't about pampering—it's about changing negative energy to positive energy," Officer Jordan asserted. "Like Mr. Williams said, '*All* students are motivated by positive statements—*no* students are motivated by negative statements.'"

"Students look up to their teachers," he continued, "Whatever their teachers communicate, they believe it. That's why it's imperative that teachers communicate positive messages. A lot of these kids don't hear positive messages at home; they sure don't hear anything positive on the street. What you say to your students today is going to influence their future. And bottom line is, their future affects your future—everyone's future—the future of our world."

Positive Teachers Inspire Students

CHAPTER 15

"As you know, your semester exam is tomorrow," Laura Nelson told her first period students Thursday morning. "You may review this period while I average your second quarter test scores. No talking!" She opened her gradebook.

At the end of first period, Julie Johnson stepped up to Laura's desk. "Excuse me, Mrs. Nelson. I was wondering about my second quarter test score average."

Laura glanced at her gradebook. "You have a C minus."

"I have a chance of passing this semester?" Julie asked.

"With an F first quarter, you'll have to pass the semester exam *and* make a passing grade on your profile paper."

Julie smiled. "I think I'll make a good grade on my paper."

Friday morning Laura Nelson's classroom wall of windows framed a dark gray sky outside.

"The grade you make on this exam counts as twenty percent of your semester grade," she said, passing out exams to her first period students.

"And how much does the profile paper count on our second quarter grade?" a student asked.

"Twenty-five percent!" Laura said.

When the bell rang two hours later, Julie Johnson was the last student to turn in her exam and profile paper. Laura looked at the title on the cover of Julie's profile folder. "*Who* is Timothy Johnson?"

"My younger brother."

Laura glared at her. "You were supposed to write about a remarkable person, not a kid brother." She picked up a red pen and scrawled a zero on the cover of Julie's folder.

Julie strapped on her faded blue backpack. "My brother may have been mentally retarded, but he *was* a remarkable person because he always smiled and he loved everyone. You never smile, Mrs. Nelson. And you don't love anyone because you don't have a heart!"

Laura opened Julie's folder after Julie stormed out of her classroom. Her eyes flooded with tears when she saw a sketch of a boy who looked like her son Michael—the same Down's syndrome features, the same winsome smile.

My brother Timothy was the most remarkable person I've ever known. Everything was special to Timothy—butterflies, birds, and bees—rainbows and rocks—pinecones and pumpkins—clouds and colored leaves—spider webs sparkling with dew. A dandelion was a rose to Timothy. An acorn was a treasure. He thought a penny made him rich. A bag of popcorn was a party. Rainy days made him happy, sunny days made him happy.

Timothy's heart was full of love. He smiled at everyone he met. He spoke to everyone he met. He hugged everyone he met.

When Timothy died, so many people besides family came to his funeral—people who said that knowing Timothy had made a difference in their lives. The neighbors came, the mailman came, clerks from the grocery store, tellers from the bank, doctors and nurses who had cared for Timothy, the ice cream man, the meter reader, the garbage man.

So many people had appreciated Timothy's special spirit. But there was a time in my life when I wished he had never been born. My dislike of Timothy started when I was five years old and he was three, when my mother brought him to my kindergarten Christmas party.

"Your brother looks funny. Is he a retard?" a classmate asked when my mother and Timothy left after the party.

"Retard, retard," several kids chanted. "Julie's brother is a dum-dum!"

"Some of the kids at school said Timothy's a retard," I told my mother when I came home that day.

"Timothy is mentally retarded, Julie," my mother said.

"Then he's dumb!" I said.

"He's not dumb, Julie. He's just different."

"I don't want a different brother. I want a regular brother!"

From the time I was five until I was thirteen, I ignored Timothy as much as possible. I shunned his love. But my heart changed one day when I was sick with strep throat. Timothy came into my bedroom, carrying his beloved old teddy bear. He tucked his bear in bed beside me and said, "Teddy wants to hug you, Julie." That day I decided I'd stop being ashamed and angry that my brother was mentally retarded. I decided I'd love Timothy for who he was instead of resenting him for who he wasn't.

I started spending time with my brother and he taught me to see beauty and magic in ordinary things. He taught me that a smile makes a difference. A positive word makes a difference. A hug makes a difference. My special brother Timothy Johnson taught me that love is more important than anything else in life.

"Love is a great teacher."

—Saint Augustine

Laura rushed to the front office. "Where's Julie Johnson this exam period?" she shouted at Leon's secretary.

"I'll see." The secretary turned to her computer screen.

Leon stepped out of his office. "Is something wrong, Mrs. Nelson?"

"I have to find Julie Johnson—I have to apologize to her!"

The secretary looked up from her computer. "Business math—Mrs. McIntosh, Room 24."

Laura barged into Room 24 without knocking. She scanned the students. "Where's Julie Johnson?" she asked Nancy McIntosh.

"Didn't show up," Nancy said.

"Didn't show up? Well, where would she be?"

Nancy frowned. "Mrs. Nelson, I don't know. Is it so important that you have to interrupt my students' exam?"

"Yes, it's important!" Laura sobbed.

"Julie left campus after first exam period," a girl said. "Told me she was walking home. Said she wasn't ever coming back to school. Seemed pretty upset," the girl said.

Laura ran back to the office. "Mr. Williams, Julie Johnson left campus after first period. A student said Julie told her she was walking home. I need Julie's address. It's urgent that I talk to her *now*—in person."

Leon looked out the office window. "It's dangerously slick out there with the sleet that's been falling the last hour." He picked up his coat. "I'll drive you, Mrs. Nelson. I know where Julie Johnson lives."

Police cars, a fire truck, an ambulance, and a towing vehicle blocked the road at the corner of Tenth Street, the street where Julie lived. Leon and Laura waited in a line of stopped traffic until the ambulance pulled away and a policeman directed them to turn left on Tenth Street to detour the accident.

"Julie!" Laura screamed when she saw a faded blue backpack lying in the ditch at the street corner. A faded blue backpack stained red.

"Julie's arms are fractured and she suffered a deep gash in her shoulder," Julie's mother spoke to Leon and Laura in the emergency waiting room. "A car that had lost control on the slick street struck Julie and knocked her into the ditch."

Mrs. Johnson shook her head. "This wouldn't have happened if Julie hadn't left school this morning. I just don't understand why she did."

Laura drew a deep breath and exhaled slowly. "I'll tell you why Julie left school, Mrs. Johnson."

Laura's eyes filled with tears when she stepped into Julie's hospital room that evening and saw Julie's broken arms—*like broken wings,* she thought.

"Mrs. Nelson! What are *you* doing here?"

"Wanting to make amends for being a heartless teacher." She placed a plush brown teddy bear beside Julie. "Delivering a teddy bear that wants to hug you."

"You read my paper!" Julie said.

"I have a son like your brother. His name's Michael. I was a positive teacher before Michael was born. But I lost my heart for stimulating students to succeed because I was angry that my mentally retarded son would never be an honor student, or play football, or graduate from high school. But you've made me see my son *is* remarkable, nonetheless. He's like your brother Timothy—always smiling, always radiating love and joy."

Julie's mother walked into the room. "Mom, this is Mrs. Nelson, my English teacher."

"We met this morning," Julie's mother said. "Mrs. Nelson told me she was quite impressed with the paper you wrote about Timothy—said you made an A plus."

"An A plus!" Julie cried, "Then I passed the semester?"

Laura smiled. "You passed the semester, Julie."

"Most of you have heard about the accident that one of our seniors, Julie Johnson, suffered last Friday morning when she was struck by a car as she was walking home after the first period exam," Laura Nelson addressed the faculty the following Monday afternoon.

"Julie Johnson left campus Friday morning because I provoked her to break—to give up academically. Because of me, Julie Johnson suffered serious physical injury. She could have suffered death. Had I been a positive teacher—helping Julie succeed instead of fostering her failure—Julie's accident wouldn't have happened."

"When I started teaching twenty years ago, I was a positive teacher—like Emily Parker. But after my son Michael was born with Down's syndrome, I had no passion for stimulating students to achieve academic success because I was resentful that Michael's academic potential was restricted by mental retardation."

"My resentment effected me not to appreciate the miracle of Michael eventually learning to read at a fifth grade level—a miracle that positive teachers at the county school for the mentally retarded have stimulated my son to achieve—positive teachers who believe *all* students can be stimulated to succeed."

"Those of you who have no passion for stimulating students to succeed, please consider a change of heart." Laura smiled and pointed to the banner *All Eagles are supposed to soar*!

POSITIVE TEACHERS
EMPOWER STUDENTS

CHAPTER 16

Graduation Day

On the last day of May, Leon Williams addressed Heritage High's seniors robed in red gowns: "You are graduating today because you put forth great academic effort to succeed. You are graduating today because particular teachers along your educational journey exerted positive energy to help you succeed."

"These positive teachers are the teachers who stimulated you to learn, encouraged you to learn, motivated you, empowered you. They gave you hope and support. They communicated positive messages that inspired you and edified you. They ministered compassion when you suffered distress."

"These positive teachers were patient and persevering, enthusiastic and attentive. These teachers smiled. These teachers are the foundation of your success today and your potential success tomorrow."

"Perpetuate in your life the positive actions and attitudes these teachers modeled and you will reach your goals, you will realize your dreams—you will 'mount up with wings as eagles'!"

Positive Teaching Formula

1. *Positive Conviction* (If you can believe, all things are possible…"—Mark 9:23)
   Objective: I will sustain faith that *all* of my students, regardless of challenges, can be stimulated to succeed.

2. *Positive Attention* ("The future is purchased by the present."—Samuel Johnson)
   Objective: I will stimulate *all* of my students to succeed.

3. *Positive Compassion* ("If I can stop one heart from breaking, I shall not live in vain."—Emily Dickinson)
   Objective: I will be a compassionate teacher.

4. *Positive Strategies* ("Teachers open the door…"—Chinese proverb)
   Objective: I will employ teaching strategies that stimulate students to learn.

5. *Positive Empowerment* ("Do the thing and you'll have the power."—Ralph Waldo Emerson)
   Objective: I will teach my students goal structuring skills which facilitate academic success.

6. *Positive Communication* ("Let no corrupt communication proceed out of your mouth, but that which is good to the use of edifying…"—Ephesians 4:29)
   Objective: I will communicate positive messages that encourage and empower my students.

POSITIVE TEACHER/
NEGATIVE TEACHER
SELF-ANALYSIS

Positive teachers employ stimulating teaching strategies. What stimulating teaching strategies do I employ?

_____

_____

_____

_____

_____

_____

_____

_____

_____

_____

_____

_____

_____

_____

_____

_____

_____

_____

_____

_____

_____

_____

_____

_____

_____

_____

_____

_____

_____

_____

_____

_____

_____

_____

_____

_____

Negative teachers subject students to academic tedium. What academic tedium, if any, do I subject my students to?

_____

_____

_____

_____

_____

_____

_____

_____

_____

_____

_____

_____

_____

_____

_____

_____

Positive teachers help students. How do I help my students succeed?

_____

_____

_____

_____

_____

_____

_____

_____

_____

_____

_____

_____

_____

_____

_____

_____

_____

Negative teachers label students. What, if any, negative labels do I affix to my students?

_____

_____

_____

_____

_____

_____

_____

_____

_____

_____

_____

_____

_____

_____

_____

_____

Positive teachers teach students. In what ways do I focus on my students' individual needs?

_____

_____

_____

_____

_____

_____

_____

_____

_____

_____

_____

_____

_____

_____

_____

Negative teachers teach curriculum. Do I focus on teaching curriculum instead of focusing on my students' individual needs? Why?

_____

_____

_____

_____

_____

_____

_____

_____

_____

_____

_____

_____

_____

_____

_____

_____

_____

_____

_____

_____

_____

_____

_____

_____

_____

_____

_____

_____

_____

_____

_____

_____

_____

_____

_____

_____

_____

Positive teachers are innovative. In what ways am I an innovative teacher?

_____

_____

_____

_____

_____

_____

_____

_____

_____

_____

_____

_____

_____

_____

_____

_____

_____

Negative teachers resist new ideas. What, if any, new ideas do I resist?

_____

_____

_____

_____

_____

_____

_____

_____

_____

_____

_____

_____

_____

_____

_____

_____

Positive teachers are positive role models. How am I a positive role model?

_____

_____

_____

_____

_____

_____

_____

_____

_____

_____

_____

_____

_____

_____

_____

Negative teachers model negative attitudes and behaviors. What, if any, negative attitudes and behaviors do I model?

_____

_____

_____

_____

_____

_____

_____

_____

_____

_____

_____

_____

_____

_____

_____

_____

Positive teachers are personable. Am I a personable teacher? How does my friendliness influence positive relationships with my students?

_____

_____

_____

_____

_____

_____

_____

_____

_____

_____

_____

_____

_____

_____

_____

Negative teachers are aloof. Am I an aloof teacher? How does this posture affect my relationship with my students?

_____

_____

_____

_____

_____

_____

_____

_____

_____

_____

_____

_____

_____

_____

_____

_____

_____

_____

_____

_____

_____

_____

_____

_____

_____

_____

_____

_____

_____

_____

_____

_____

_____

_____

_____

Positive teachers are compassionate. How do I reflect compassion to my students?

_____

_____

_____

_____

_____

_____

_____

_____

_____

_____

_____

_____

_____

_____

_____

_____

_____

_____

_____

_____

_____

_____

_____

_____

_____

_____

_____

_____

_____

_____

_____

_____

_____

_____

_____

_____

_____

Negative teachers are condescending. When, if ever, have I been condescending to a student, or students?

_____

_____

_____

_____

_____

_____

_____

_____

_____

_____

_____

_____

_____

_____

_____

_____

Positive teachers listen. How has listening to my students' problems and concerns affected a positive difference?

_____

_____

_____

_____

_____

_____

_____

_____

_____

_____

_____

_____

_____

_____

_____

_____

Negative teachers turn away. When, if ever, have I turned away a student, or students, who needed my attention?

_____

_____

_____

_____

_____

_____

_____

_____

_____

_____

_____

_____

_____

_____

_____

Positive teachers are patient. How do I practice patience with my students?

_____

_____

_____

_____

_____

_____

_____

_____

_____

_____

_____

_____

_____

_____

Negative teachers are quick-tempered. Do I sometimes lose my temper with my students? How could I control my anger instead of losing my temper?

_____

_____

_____

_____

_____

_____

_____

_____

_____

_____

_____

_____

_____

_____

_____

_____

_____

Positive teachers inspire students. How do I inspire my students?

_____

_____

_____

_____

_____

_____

_____

_____

_____

_____

_____

_____

_____

_____

_____

_____

_____

Negative teachers intimidate students. Have I ever intimidated a student, or students? Did my intimidation stimulate a positive outcome?

_____

_____

_____

_____

_____

_____

_____

_____

_____

_____

_____

_____

_____

_____

_____

_____

_____

_____

Positive teachers praise. Do I praise my students? Do I praise *all* of my students, or particular students? Do I praise *all* positive actions and behaviors, or only positive performance related to academics?

_____

_____

_____

_____

_____

_____

_____

_____

_____

_____

_____

_____

_____

_____

_____

Negative teachers criticize. Do I criticize my students? What behaviors, actions, or performance do I criticize? Does my criticism generate positive change?

_____

_____

_____

_____

_____

_____

_____

_____

_____

_____

_____

_____

_____

_____

_____

_____

Positive teachers practice behavior modification. What behavior modification techniques do I practice?

_____

_____

_____

_____

_____

_____

_____

_____

_____

_____

_____

_____

_____

_____

_____

Negative teachers administer punishment. Do I punish my students? What punishments do I administer? Do the punishments I administer generate positive change?

Positive teachers smile. What positive messages do I communicate to my students when I smile?

_____

_____

_____

_____

_____

_____

_____

_____

_____

_____

_____

_____

_____

_____

Negative teachers frown. What negative messages do I communicate to my students when I frown?

_____

_____

_____

_____

_____

_____

_____

_____

_____

_____

_____

_____

_____

_____

_____

_____

Positive teachers encourage. How do I encourage my students?

_____

_____

_____

_____

_____

_____

_____

_____

_____

_____

_____

_____

_____

_____

_____

Negative teachers discourage. Have I ever discouraged a student, or students? What discouraging message(s) did I communicate to my student(s)?

_____

_____

_____

_____

_____

_____

_____

_____

_____

_____

_____

_____

_____

_____

_____

Positive teachers are flexible. How do I practice flexibility in the classroom?

_____

_____

_____

_____

_____

_____

_____

_____

_____

_____

_____

_____

_____

Negative teachers are rigid. When, if ever, have I been an unyielding teacher in a situation where change or modification would benefit my student(s)?

_____

_____

_____

_____

_____

_____

_____

_____

_____

_____

_____

_____

_____

_____

_____

_____

Positive teachers don't waste instructional time. How do I accomplish making every school day count as a day of learning?

_____

_____

_____

_____

_____

_____

_____

_____

_____

_____

_____

_____

_____

_____

_____

_____

_____

Negative teachers assign busywork. Do I sometimes assign my students busywork? What kind of nonproductive work do I assign, and why?

_____

_____

_____

_____

_____

_____

_____

_____

_____

_____

_____

_____

_____

_____

_____

_____

Positive teachers express enthusiasm. How do I express enthusiasm?

_____

_____

_____

_____

_____

_____

_____

_____

_____

_____

_____

_____

_____

_____

_____

_____

Negative teachers express indifference. When, if ever, have I expressed indifference?

_____

_____

_____

_____

_____

_____

_____

_____

_____

_____

_____

_____

_____

_____

_____

_____

_____

_____

Positive teachers motivate students. How do I motivate my students?

_____

_____

_____

_____

_____

_____

_____

_____

_____

_____

_____

_____

_____

_____

_____

Negative teachers suppress students. Have I ever suppressed a student, or students? How?

_____

_____

_____

_____

_____

_____

_____

_____

_____

_____

_____

_____

_____

_____

_____

_____

Positive teachers use positive language. What positive messages do I communicate to my students?

_____

_____

_____

_____

_____

_____

_____

_____

_____

_____

_____

_____

_____

_____

_____

Negative teachers use negative language. What negative messages, if any, do I communicate to my students?

_____

_____

_____

_____

_____

_____

_____

_____

_____

_____

_____

_____

_____

_____

_____

_____

Positive teachers persevere. Do I believe *all* students can be stimulated to succeed? Why?

_____

_____

_____

_____

_____

_____

_____

_____

_____

_____

_____

_____

_____

_____

_____

_____

Negative teachers give up. Have I ever given up on stimulating a student, or students, to succeed? Why?

_____

_____

_____

_____

_____

_____

_____

_____

_____

_____

_____

_____

_____

_____

_____

Positive teachers care. How do I show my students that I care?

_____

_____

_____

_____

_____

_____

_____

_____

_____

_____

_____

_____

_____

_____

_____

_____

_____

_____

Negative teachers are unconcerned. Am I a calloused teacher? Why?

_____

_____

_____

_____

_____

_____

_____

_____

_____

_____

_____

_____

_____

_____

_____

_____

Positive teachers nurture students. How do I nurture my students?

_____

_____

_____

_____

_____

_____

_____

_____

_____

_____

_____

_____

_____

_____

_____

_____

Negative teachers neglect students. Have I ever neglected a student, or students? Why?

_____

_____

_____

_____

_____

_____

_____

_____

_____

_____

_____

_____

_____

_____

_____

_____

_____

Positive teachers empower students. How do I empower my students?

_____

_____

_____

_____

_____

_____

_____

_____

_____

_____

_____

_____

_____

_____

_____

_____

Negative teachers fail students. How many students have I failed in the years I've been teaching? What could I have done to stimulate these students to succeed?

_____

_____

_____

_____

_____

_____

_____

_____

_____

_____

_____

_____

_____

_____

_____

_____

Why did I become a teacher?

_____

_____

_____

_____

_____

_____

_____

_____

What are my primary teaching objectives?

_____

_____

_____

_____

_____

_____

_____

_____

How would my students describe me as a teacher?

_____

_____

_____

_____

_____

_____

_____

_____

How would I describe myself as a teacher?

_____

_____

_____

_____

_____

_____

_____

_____

_____

"To teach is to touch a life forever." If today were my last opportunity to make a positive difference in the lives of my students, what would my lesson plan be? What teaching strategies would I employ? What attitudes would I reflect? What messages would I communicate? What would be my final statement before my students left my classroom forever?

_____

_____

_____

_____

_____

_____

_____

_____

_____

_____

_____

_____

_____

_____

Afterword

Our nation's school systems promote special academic programs, computer curriculum, and state of the art facilities as solutions to stimulating students to succeed. But these promotions aren't working for *all* students; they never have and they never will. Until we have positive teachers in every classroom in every school, *all* students will not reach their academic potential. Until we have teachers who believe every student is bright and can be stimulated to succeed—teachers who make every school day count—teachers who employ positive teaching strategies—teachers who are compassionate—teachers who teach success skills—and teachers who practice positive communication—multitudes of students will continue to fail, and multitudes of students will continue to drop out of school.

When I tutored the young man who had dropped out of school and then failed the GED exam, I tutored him at a kitchen table—no special academic program for challenged students, no computer curriculum. When I tutored my grandson who had failed eighth grade, I tutored him at a kitchen table—no special academic program for challenged students, no computer curriculum. And yet both students were stimulated to learn and achieve academic success.

I've taught students in old classrooms with old desks and tattered textbooks—I've taught students in new classrooms with new desks and new textbooks—and I know from years of teaching experience that positive teaching postures, not the quality or condition of academic facilities, are the stimuli that influence student success.

Computer curriculum isn't a viable substitute for the personal attention of positive teachers. Computers don't smile. Computers aren't compassionate. Computers don't reflect enthusiasm. Computers don't encourage, motivate, praise, inspire, and empower students. Computers don't stimulate students to succeed.

Special academic programs are only as effective as the teachers who teach them. Too many of our students are spending years in special education classes and still not succeeding academically. I know a bright young man who was in special education classes for six years, from seventh grade through twelfth grade. He graduated with an attendance diploma, still deficient in basic academic skills.

When my son was in third grade, he was placed in a gifted program; a year later, I withdrew him from the program. While I wasn't an authority of gifted programs, I did discern that the teacher of the program wasn't gifted, just as some special education teachers aren't special—just as many teachers aren't positive.

I wasn't a positive teacher when I started teaching. I had good intentions—I had the desire to be a positive teacher—but no positive teaching training. I knew how to teach subject material, but I didn't know how to stimulate students to learn. Real-life classroom experience promptly taught me that traditional teaching postures—most of which are negative in nature—don't stimulate students to learn, especially challenged students.

A seed of positive teaching awareness was sown by a positive principal, Jim Scott, who told me, and my new teacher colleagues, that the primary priority of effective teaching is to always consider the humanistic factor when working with students. From this seed of awareness, I began to practice positive conviction, positive attention, positive compassion, positive strategies, positive empowerment, and positive communication.

I would like to say that I practiced positive teaching postures one hundred percent of the time, but I didn't. I would like to say that I stimulated *all* of my students to succeed, but I didn't. But I do know from long-term teaching experience that positive teaching postures *can* stimulate any student to succeed.

I also know from experience that when our students leave our classroom at the end of the school year, our opportunity to stimulate a positive difference in their lives is terminated. Regrets cannot be redeemed after the final bell; failures cannot be resurrected. Those students who leave our classroom without having realized success take us with them, for we are a part of their failure.

And those students who leave our classroom having realized success take us with them, for we have touched all of their tomorrows with a positive impression.

"To teach is to touch a life forever."

About the Author

Jeannie Wunsch / R & W Photo 2002

Janice Farley graduated cum laude from Florida Southern College in 1981. She taught high school English in Florida for fourteen years; in

1994 she was selected to be listed in "Who's Who Among America's Teachers."

Her graduate studies include advanced writing (University of Central Florida), self-esteem for educators (Jacksonville University—Florida), and educational research (North Georgia College and State University). She currently holds a Georgia Educator Certificate.

Janice, a native Floridian, lives with her husband in North Georgia. She has written two novels, short stories, essays, and poetry. She is presently writing a book on life lessons.

0-595-26241-4

Printed in the United States
40039LVS00004B/179

9 780595 262410